THE CRIME AT DIANA'S POOL

Victor L. Whitechurch

Spitfire Publishers

CONTENTS

ABOUT 'THE CRIME AT DIANA'S POOL'

The Pleasaunce was a fine country house nestling below the hills which flanked the picturesque village of Coppleswick, deep in southern England. Today, its new owner, mysterious ex-diplomat Felix Nayland is playing host to the county worthies. The lavish summer garden party laid on to introduce Felix and his sister Alice to the community is in full swing. The Green Albanian Band and Western Glee Singers are entertaining Nayland's guests including young local vicar, Harry Westerham and Major Challow, the Chief Constable of Downshire. Leaving the party the Vicar and Major take a shortcut through the estate's water garden and make a horrifying discovery – a man lying face down dead in an ornamental pool. A knife embedded deep in his back. The shrewd and observant Vicar turns amateur sleuth ably assisting the industrious Detective Sergeant Ringwood.

About the Author

Victor Lorenzo Whitechurch was a Church of England clergyman and noted English crime novelist. He was born in Norham, Northumberland in 1868 and trained to be a vicar at Chichester Theological College and Durham University. Relatively late in life Victor became rather infatuated with the detective novel and between 1912 and 1932 wrote eight, many centred around the fictional South Downs cathedral and university city of Frattenbury, and often featuring members of the clergy. He was one of the founding members of the Detection Club and contributed to the Club's collaborative novel *The Floating Admiral*, published in 1931, which also featured Agatha Christie Dorothy L. Sayers, and G.K. Chesterton. His most famous literary creation however, is amateur railway detective Thorpe Hazelle, a wealthy, vegetarian fitness fanatic who starred in *Thrilling Stories of the Railway* (recently dramatized for BBC Radio 4 and featuring Benedict Cumberbatch). Ellery Queen described Hazelle as 'the first of the speciality detectives'. Another was the young detective clergyman, Reverend Harry Westerham, who appeared in *The Crime at Diana's Pool*, described by Martin Edwards in *The Story of Classic Crime in 100 Books* as 'A quintessentially English country-house mystery with a touch of the exotic.' Victor Whitechurch died in 1933, aged 65.

Praise for Victor L. Whitechurch

The Crime at Diana's Pool
'Quite charming... devotees of mystery yarns will enjoy this story'
New York Times
'A quintessentially English country-house mystery with a touch of the exotic'
Martin Edwards, The Story of Classic Crime in 100 Books
'A model of the detective story... the solution has the neatness of a bold mate at chess'
Glasgow Herald
'Excellent'
Dorothy L. Sayers
'A good job of murder'
Barzun & Taylor, A Catalogue of Crime

Thrilling Stories of the Railway
'All Whitechurch's stories have distinct merit'
Barzun & Taylor, A Catalogue of Crime
'The first of the speciality detectives'

Ellery Queen
'His most highly regarded work in the crime genre'
Martin Edwards

Shot on the Downs
'Whitechurch's writing was of a higher quality than that of many other detective novelists of his time'
Martin Edwards, The Story of Classic Crime in 100 Books

The Robbery at Rudwick House
'A very entertaining yarn'
New York Times

Murder at Exbridge
'Should delight those who take pleasure in pitting their analytical abilities against those of the sleuth created by the author'
New York Times

Murder at the Pageant
'Enthralling... keeps the reader keenly interested'
Boston Transcript
'Victor Whitechurch is at his best in *Murder at the Pageant*'
The Sunday Times

The Dean and Jecinora
'A novel of exceptional charm'
The Scotsman

The Templeton Case
'A straight detective story... the reader has a fair chance to beat the detective to the solution'
New York Times

FOREWORD

If it is permitted to dignify what is merely a detective yarn with a preface I should like to tell the reader a little secret about the method on which the tale is constructed. In most detective stories the author knows exactly what the end is going to be, and writes up to that end from the beginning. But, in reality, the solver of a problem in criminology has to begin at the beginning, without knowing the end, working it out from clues concerning which he does not recognise the full bearing at first.

I have tried to follow this method in the construction of the following story. To begin with I had no plot. When I had written the first chapter I did not know why the crime had been committed, who had done it, or how it was done. Then, with an open mind, I picked up the clues which seemed to show themselves, and found, as I went on, their bearing on the problem. In many respects the story appeared to work itself out to that inevitable conclusion about which, to begin with, I was in entire ignorance.

A speculative reader may, if he chooses, close the book when he has read the first chapter, and try to evolve a plot from what he finds there. It would be interesting to know if his conclusions resemble, in any way, what follows in the book.

Victor L. Whitechurch

CHAPTER 1

When Mr Felix Nayland bought "The Pleasaunce" at Coppleswick and came into residence there with an unmarried sister who kept house for him there was a little flutter of excitement, not only in the village of Coppleswick, but in the surrounding neighbourhood. Who *was* Felix Nayland? Are people calling at "The Pleasaunce?" For Coppleswick was situated in one of those favoured areas which are known by the name of "residential neighbourhoods," and at least two of the families living there were in the County set.

Coppleswick was six miles from the County Town of Sydbury, and although in the changing times the society of the sleepy old town included men who journeyed the forty odd miles to London daily, and a sprinkling of new rich who formed a contrast with the older inhabitants, still there remained a select few of the latter who asked the same question, "should they call on these new people at Coppleswick?"

The matter was soon settled, however, by those who had every right to settle it, Major Challow, the Chief Constable of the County, who resided at Sydbury, and Sir Frank Gifford, whose family had occupied Coppleswick Hall for centuries. And the matter was settled for *them* in the first instance by old General Torrington—in a certain London Club to which all three belonged. The General knew, or knew about, everyone who ought to be known, and, when appealed to, said,

"Nayland? Felix Nayland? Oh, yes. He's all right. Worcestershire people. I knew an uncle of his years ago—in one of the Gladstonian Cabinets—Foreign Office, I think. Felix

Nayland was in the Diplomatic service for a time—then he went abroad on his own account—fond of exploring, I fancy—but I never heard much about what he did. His sister's a charming woman—engaged to poor young Littledean who was killed in the late nineties in an Alpine accident. She never married. Living with him at Coppleswick, is she? Oh, certainly—call on them by all means."

"What sort of a fellow is he?" asked Major Challow.

"I only saw him once, when he was quite young. He'd be about fifty today. Rather reserved, I remember,—clever—bit of a sportsman—he got his blue at Oxford—but, as I've told you, he's been abroad for some time. His sister has been living at Eastbourne, and I've frequently met her. There's a bit of money, but not very much, I fancy. Felix Nayland was a younger son."

So Major Challow and Sir Frank Gifford called, with their respective wives, on Felix Nayland and his sister, the pioneers of a steady little stream of callers whose cards mounted up to a respectable pile in an antique silver filigree basket on the hall table at "The Pleasaunce"; and the result was the usual dinners, teas, and at homes.

And then, in the middle of a glorious summer, came the garden party at "The Pleasaunce," and cards of invitation were issued over the surrounding neighbourhood, cards which caused a mild flutter of excitement because in one corner of them appeared the legend,—"The Green Albanian Band and Western Glee Singers." These cards were sent out a good three weeks before the event, and everybody who was anybody duly displayed them on their mantelpieces—as reminders.

"The Pleasaunce" nestled below the hills which flanked one side of Coppleswick, it stood well away from the main road from which it was reached by a narrow lane of some two hundred yards in length, curving, abruptly, just before it led to the front of the house. The house itself was not very large, but stood in good sized grounds, wooded rather thickly on the level part of them at the back of the house, but open around the building itself.

A curve of the drive brought one to the front of "The Pleasaunce," half a dozen steps to the hall door, and on either side of these steps was a paved terrace on to which the French windows of the front rooms opened. Just beyond the house, and at the side of it, was a fair sized lawn, which, at the moment, was set out with tea tables and chairs. In one corner stood a small marquee, from which the tea and other refreshments were to be served, and in another corner a piano and portable music-stands. The reception was so arranged that the guests first mounted the steps and were received by the host and hostess, and then, naturally, passed along the terrace and so drifted on to the lawn.

Felix Nayland fulfilled General Torrington's hazard as to his age. He was evidently about fifty, a thin, spare man, with small moustache and little, pointed beard—both of them tinged with grey. His rather dark face had a wrinkled, weather-beaten expression, his eyes were slightly sunken, though their glance, as he welcomed each guest, was keen. He was dressed in a well cut navy-blue suit, and wore a Panama.

Miss Nayland was shorter and stouter—evidently the elder of the two. Her hair was quite white. She had an extremely pleasant face, smiling as she shook hands with the stream of arrivals.

"I *do* hope it will keep fine, dear Miss Nayland," exclaimed Mrs Leigh-Hulcott, a fussy little woman, "We've all been looking forward to it *so* much—and now the weather seems inclined to change. It *is* a shame!"

"Oh, I don't think it will rain before night," said Nayland, looking, however, a little apprehensively at some dark clouds which were gathering on the horizon.

"Rotten luck if it does—what!" exclaimed Major Challow, who came up at that moment. The Chief Constable was a typical military man, tall, back upright, with a queer little swaggering movement of his shoulders when he walked, faultlessly dressed in a light grey suit and Homburg hat. He was accompanied by his wife and daughter.

"Did you drive over, Major?" asked Miss Nayland, who knew he prided himself on his handling of his new Napier.

"Not today. My man ran us here. I have to go to Marton by train later on—from the station here—so he'll take my wife and daughter home. Ah—how are you, Miss Garforth?"

"Topping, thanks. Do tell me, Major, are these men real Albanians? I thought Albanians had white hair and pink eyes, and I'm frightfully disappointed."

Major Challow laughed as he strolled on to the lawn with his companion, a bright, up-to-date girl, with merry, laughing grey eyes, the daughter of a barrister who lived in the neighbourhood. "You're thinking of Albinos, aren't you," he replied, "but I don't suppose these fellows in green are Albanians any more than the Blue Hungarians are particularly continental, only they're precious smart—what!"

Out of a French window on the side of the house, opening directly on to the lawn, came the Band, carrying their instruments, a small room having been made over to them for dressing purposes. Their distinguishing feature, as their name implied, took the form of a dark green jacket, with silver collar and cuffs. Apparently this jacket was the sum total of their uniforms, for each of them wore ordinary nondescript trousers beneath it, while, if they possessed any particular headgear, it was not in evidence, for they were bare headed. There were eight of them in number, a pianist, two violinists, a 'cello, a bass, a cornet player, a performer on various instruments consisting of small drum, triangle, cymbals, and bells, and the Conductor, whose jacket bore gold collar and cuffs instead of silver, and who, as he walked across the lawn, carried a violin and a piccolo as well as his baton.

"Jove, though," went on the Major, adjusting his monocle as he spoke, "one of 'em's a foreigner, apparently, even if he isn't a pink eyed white rabbit, Miss Garforth. I mean the fiddler with the black beard."

"*I see*," replied Miss Garforth, "the man whose coat doesn't fit him—it's a bit too big. Oh, yes—he doesn't look English, does he?"

The bandsmen seated themselves, or stood in front of their stands, and the Conductor distributed music sheets, looked round, tapped his stand with his baton to call them to attention, and the next moment was vigorously beating time while they struck up an operatic selection. At once it became evident that the Green Albanian Band, whatever its nationality, was of the first order. People even paused in their conversation to listen—a rare compliment from an English audience.

The lawn was crowded now. Guests were seating themselves at the tea tables or standing in little groups. Waiters and waitresses came out of the refreshment marquee bearing trays —under the direction of an individual who did nothing himself, but kept an alert eye on those who served, a dark, clean-shaven man of about forty years of age whose very attitude as he stood at the entrance of the marquee proclaimed the well trained butler.

Major Challow was in his element. He loved social functions and prided himself on his nice manners. To equals he was on an equality, to those whom he considered a trifle beneath his standing he was, perhaps unconsciously, just a wee bit condescending; to superiors—but superiors did not often come within the limit of his range of mental vision.

He had come back to the edge of the terrace, and stood there, coffee cup in hand, surveying the crowded lawn from the slight eminence. He liked to know who was there and who was not there at any function, and he had the gift of remembering everyone.

"How d'ye do, Major!"

Major Challow turned towards the man who accosted him, a clergyman, wearing a dark grey suit and straw hat, a man of about thirty, not very tall, squarely built, clean shaven, with a good humoured, pleasant face—dark brown eyes with an occasional twinkle in them—the Vicar of Coppleswick.

"Hullo, Westerham," replied the Major "I was wondering if you'd be here. I rather wanted to see you."

"What about, Major?"

"Well, it's a matter I can't very well discuss here—concerns one of your parishioners. Look here, I've got to take the six forty-five train from Coppleswick to Marton. Could you give me twenty minutes later on."

"All right. We can slip away from this and go to the Vicarage—soon after six?"

"That'll do capitally. Jove, Nayland's collected a crowd, what! There are several people here I've never seen before. Who's that fellow over there—near the Band—in the brown suit?"

"Don't know. Quite a stranger to me. Some of the people have brought friends who are staying with them. Well, I'll go and make myself pleasant—and get a cup of tea, if I can. See you later."

Guests who had finished tea were making a move through a gateway on the further side of the lawn, Felix Nayland leading the way.

"We *must* go and see the garden," said Mrs Leigh-Hulcott to a friend, "haven't you seen it, dear? Oh, it's *most* extraordinary. He calls it a garden, you know, but it's really a weird kind of wilderness. It quite gives one the *creeps*—especially if the sun isn't shining. But he's *frightfully* proud of it. Come along."

They strolled along the mown grass path that led through a small paddock to the "garden." Mrs Leigh-Hulcott was right. The place was very weird, especially just then in the gathering gloom, for the threatening rain clouds were slowly rolling up and obscuring the sky. The "garden" consisted of an area of irregular ground, merging into a wood, the trees of which were at first scattered, gradually becoming more dense. Winding around these trees were a succession of grass paths, all of which finally converged to a piece of water. A small stream, running through the wood, had been artificially dammed so that two natural hollows, one below the other, had been formed into deep pools of water. A narrow grass path divided these pools, that on the right hand was almost on a level with the path, while the surface of the left hand pool was several feet below it, at the foot of a steep grassy bank.

Around the upper pool rocks had been arranged, between which were growing the characteristic plants of a water garden. In the lower pool were masses of water lilies, except just in one spot where the water was apparently very deep. Beyond these pools the path which separated them continued through the wood, winding sinuously amid its depths.

"Yes," said Felix Nayland, as he stood on the path between the pools, "it is a little out of the common, isn't it?" And he spoke with pride to the little group of guests, "I wish the sun was out, so that you could see the effect of the shadows. I call this," and he pointed down the steep bank, "Diana's pool."

"I hope you don't expect me to put on a bathing dress and disport myself in it!" said Miss Garforth.

"Why?" asked Nayland.

"Because, you see, my name happens to be Diana," said the girl, with a laugh in which they all joined, "Ugh!" and she gave a little shudder, "I shouldn't care to! It looks so frightfully gloomy!"

Nayland shook his head.

"I'm sorry," he said "the sunshine would make all the difference—I—"

"There!" broke in Mrs Leigh-Hulcott "I felt a spot of rain! I was afraid it would come. It *is* hard luck, Mr Nayland—and everything has been *so* delightful."

"Never mind," replied Nayland, "We'll cheat the weather yet. I've arranged for the Glee Singers to give their entertainment inside—in the hall—if it's wet. We'd better go back to the house and take shelter. I think you'll like them."

A few drops of rain began to fall as they hurried back. Miss Nayland was announcing to the guests on the lawn that the glees would be sung in the hall. The bandsmen were having their tea in the marquee, having put their instruments into their room. The gardener and a couple of other men were preparing to carry the piano into the hall: Nayland went to them to give directions and then made for the front door, calling upon his guests to follow. He was the first to enter the hall, the Vicar following close upon him.

Nayland gave a little start as he went inside the house into the hall. Standing on the further side and the only occupant, with his back to the door, was the bandsman with the black beard whom Major Challow had pointed out to Diana Garforth. He turned, suddenly, as the two men came in, looked slightly confused, and then said, in a soft toned voice with a trace of a foreign accent in it,

"I hope I do not intrude, sir? I was admiring these beautiful things."

All around the hall was a collection of curiosities, a couple of heavy Corean chests with massive brass work, lacquered Chinese cabinets, trophies of Indian and South American weapons displayed on the walls, the usual collection of a connoisseur who had travelled much and brought mementos home with him.

For a moment or two Felix Nayland stood silent, looking intently at the man wearing the green jacket. But the men carrying the piano, followed by the guests, crowded in behind him, and he had only time to give vent to a curt:

"Oh, all right."

The bandsman came quickly across the hall and, with some difficulty, edged his way out through the throng of incoming guests, glancing furtively at Nayland as he did so. And Nayland, for a moment, returned the glance, keenly. But the chatter of conversation and the arrival of the Glee Singers, who came from an inside entrance, diverted all attention.

Nayland and the Vicar were standing just inside the open hall door when the concert commenced. The latter spoke a word or two to his host, but Nayland seemed to be a bit preoccupied, and presently slipped out of the door through the little group who were listening outside, under the shelter of the verandah which covered the terrace.

After a bit, Westerham, who was not particularly musical, and craved for a smoke, went out on to the terrace. In deference to the occasion he had previously been smoking cigarettes, which he despised, and this was the opportunity for a quiet pipe. He filled and lighted his pipe and glanced at his watch. A quarter to six. He remembered his appointment with Major Challow—just after six. He strolled to the edge of the terrace and looked out on the now deserted lawn. The rain, which up till then had been falling in desultory drops, was increasing. It was evidently setting in for a wet evening. The clouds were thick and black and the whole aspect dreary in the extreme.

Looking around lazily over the paddock to the "garden" beyond he noticed, very indistinctly, someone moving within the outer trees. It was so dark there that he could not see at all plainly, and was not sure if there were two or only one figure. It was only afterwards on concentrating his thoughts, that he remembered that he fancied he caught sight of something green with a flash of metal on it. But, just then, he had no particular reason for any suspicion. He paced up and down the terrace two or three times, and then, in spite of the rain—for it was well known that the Vicar was impervious to weather—went out on the lawn to get a better view of the clouding sky. Round the corner of the house he heard voices and looked casually through the open window into the bandsmen's room. Whiskey, soda water siphons and glasses stood on the table, and the bandsmen were enjoying these refreshments of heavier type while they packed their instruments. Some of them were putting on light rain coats over their gaudy green jackets—evidently preparing to start.

By this time the rain was coming down in torrents. Westerham took shelter for a few minutes inside the marquee, where the waiters were packing crockery. The butler came in, his black coat splashed with rain.

"Can I get you anything, sir?"

"No thanks. What unfortunate weather!"

"It is, indeed, sir."

Then Westerham crossed to the terrace once more. The Glee Singers had finished their performance, the guests were departing, in a confusion of rain and motors. Miss Nayland stood just outside the open door, bidding farewells. Her brother was nowhere to be seen.

"He went out half way through the concert," said Westerham, "I haven't set eyes on him since."

"How naughty of him—when he ought to be taking leave of his guests. Goodbye, Mrs Lambourne. *So* sorry it's turned out like this. Yes? What is it?"

The Conductor of the Band had come up.

"There's a private bus to take you all to the station," went on Miss Nayland. "Thank you so much. The music was delightful— Yes?"

"We can't find one of our men, madam," said the Conductor, "His overcoat is in the room we have been using—and his violin. It's rather awkward. We can't wait for him! We must catch this train as we have an engagement in London tonight."

"How very tiresome," replied Miss Nayland. "When did you see him last?"

"Was he the one with the beard?" broke in the Vicar, who was standing near.

"Yes. We haven't seen him since we had our tea."

"He was here a little while ago," said Westerham.

"I'm afraid he must find his own way now," said the Conductor. "How about his overcoat and violin?"

"Oh, leave them," said Miss Nayland, good-naturedly, "if he turns up soon someone will run him down to the station, and he may catch the train after all. Good afternoon—and very many thanks. Ah, Goodbye, Mrs Challow. I hope you won't be any the worse for this unlucky day."

"Now then, padre," said the Major, turning to the Vicar, "if you can give me a few minutes—what! Beastly weather—yes—I've got a coat."

"There's a short cut to the Vicarage through the wood," said Westerham, "and it'll be a bit sheltered under the trees."

"Good! You lead the way."

The two men walked across the lawn, through the gate into the paddock, hurrying across the open space, and reached the partly sheltered "garden", their feet sinking into the now sodden grass paths. Westerham was leading the way across the narrow path between the two pools, when he suddenly stopped, and uttered an exclamation of horror. At the same moment the Major, who had caught sight of what his companion had seen, cried out,

"Good God—what's that?"

In the pool below them—the pool on the left—was a blurred mass of green with a silver glint beneath the water, while on the edge of the bank were two feet, the soles of the boots uppermost.

"Must have stumbled and pitched headlong into it!" exclaimed Westerham, scrambling down the steep bank, followed by the Major, "No wonder they missed him! I hope we're in time— artificial respiration—perhaps—ah—"

The man was lying on his face, all under water except for his feet and the lower part of his legs. Seizing these they slowly pulled him up.

"Look!" suddenly cried the Major, as the upper part of the body came into view.

"What?"

Then Westerham saw.

Beneath the man's shoulder blades, a little to the left, stuck out a short, black thing, with a metal top. The handle of a knife.

"It's murder!" gasped the Major as, between them, they managed to hoist him to the top of the bank, a heavy, dripping inert mass, still lying on his face.

"I wonder who he—" began the Vicar, as, slowly, they turned him over on his side. Then both men uttered a fresh exclamation of horror. The face of the man was not that of the black bearded bandsman whose jacket he was wearing. The man they had found stabbed in the back and lying in Diana's pool was their host—Felix Nayland!

CHAPTER 2

The Chief Constable was the first to pull himself together after the few moments of surprised silence which elapsed. He recognised that he must act immediately, and in an official capacity.

"It can only have happened within the last half hour," he said. "When did you see poor Nayland last, padre?"

"He went out of the hall—and about ten minutes afterwards I looked at my watch. It was then a quarter to six. It's now a quarter past."

"Good heavens," replied the Major, "the man that drove that knife into him can't have got far. We must follow this up at once."

He glanced round for a moment, and shrugged his shoulders.

"Any amount of people been about here this afternoon, what!"

"Yes," replied the Vicar, "but not since it rained heavily—if you're thinking of impressions."

"Gad, but you're right," interrupted the Major. "We must see to that. Now look here: Do you think anyone is likely to come along and disturb things?"

"I should hardly imagine so."

"Very well. We must leave him as he is for the present. Is 'The Pleasaunce' on the telephone?"

"Yes."

"Then while I get on to my men at Sydbury, you must break the news to Miss Nayland—a beastly job, what! But it's got to be done and it's more in your line than mine. Then, if you don't mind, I want you to come back here and watch till I send someone—

I'll get hold of my man here, Froome, the village policeman. Of course we'll have a detective out from Sydbury immediately, but I don't want to chance anything till he comes."

The two men were now hurrying back to the house. The Vicar said,

"I suppose you'll be telephoning this bandsman's description to Sydbury, Major?"

"Of course," replied the Chief Constable, a little shortly. He was not a man to be approached by an outsider when engaged in his work.

"Because, if I may suggest it," went on the Vicar, "as Nayland is, somehow or other, wearing his jacket it's just on the cards that he's wearing Nayland's;—dark navy blue, two buttons on the wrist. And he had on a pair of very dark grey trousers with a suspicion of thin black stripes, brown shoes, with crepe soles, and I caught a glimpse of his tie under his beard—light violet—sort of lilac."

Major Challow looked intently at the Vicar for a moment, and said,

"Gad! Padre. You're pretty observant, what!"

"It's a hobby of mine," replied the clergyman.

The butler opened the door to them when they reached the house, looking at them inquiringly.

"I want to see your mistress," said Westerham, "and Major Challow wishes to use the telephone."

"And do you know where Froome lives?" asked the Major.

"The policeman? Yes, sir."

"Will you please send for him at once—tell him I want him, and ask him to come here for me."

"Yes, sir—certainly—excuse me, sir—is anything the matter?"

"Yes," replied the Major. "I will tell you presently. Who are you sending for Froome?"

"The gardener is in the kitchen, sir. He can go."

"Very well. And, look here. I don't want anyone else to leave the house till I've seen them—you as well. Understand, what! See to it, will you please."

"Very good, sir—Miss Nayland is in the drawing room," he added to Westerham, opening the door and announcing him. "This way, sir," he went on to the Major. "The telephone is in the library."

And the Major, as soon as he was in that particular room closed and locked the door. Then he rang up police headquarters at Sydbury, gave a long stream of short concise orders, looked at his watch, and said to himself,

"I shall have to go to Marton some other time—this is a bigger affair. Gad, yes!"

Meanwhile Westerham was discharging his very difficult task of breaking the terrible news to Miss Nayland. He was a keen judge of character and felt instinctively that it was a case which would permit of no beating about the bush, with mysterious hints of an accident and the raising of any false hopes. Very quietly and sympathetically he asked Miss Nayland to prepare herself to receive very bad news, and proceeded, in an equally quiet and sympathetic manner to tell her exactly what had happened.

As he had thought, he found her very brave. After the first shock she broke down a little, and he remained silent. Then, as she partly recovered herself, he said a few simple words of consolation. She bowed her head.

"You are very kind, Mr Westerham—indeed, I know you well enough to believe you would be—I am glad that it is you who have told me this terrible thing. You must forgive me if I don't say much,—but it has numbed me—only—is there anything I can do?"

"I don't think so—just now," he replied. "May I come in by and by and see you? Later on I'm afraid you will have to give the police information. Can I help you?"

"When—when will they bring him?"

"Presently. There are things to be done first."

"I should like to see him."

"You shall. I will be here and will let you know. I think you would rather I left you now?"

She nodded.

He went out of the room quietly and prepared to return to the scene of the tragedy. Suddenly, however, he crossed the hall—to the spot where he and Nayland had seen the bandsman standing with his back to them when they had come in to prepare for the Glee Singers. It was just in front of one of the large Corean chests.

He stood there with knitted brows. He was a pretty frequent visitor at "The Pleasaunce" for the esteem between himself and his new parishioner had been mutual. He was trying to remember occasions when Nayland had talked about some of the curiosities the hall contained. He had acknowledged to Major Challow that he was an observant man, and this was true. He had made it a habit of practising registering things in his mind, a useful habit, as every parish priest knows who has tried it. Over and over again in the course of house to house visiting in his parish some object, lying on the table, or mantelpiece, would bring back to his mind in a flash the recollection of a former visit, and he would be able to ask, by association of ideas, whether Mary was getting on in her new place, what had happened to Tom since he had joined the Army, or had Mrs Bunce had another attack of rheumatism—things which had passed out of his mind between the visits, to be recalled by a pair of brass candlesticks, an old clock, or the cartwheel pattern on the back of a wooden chair.

Now he tried to reverse the process—by making an effort to recollect the last conversation he had had with Felix Nayland when they had stood together in front of that Corean chest. What was it? Ah—it was coming—Nayland had told him a yarn connected with that Mexican knife hanging on the wall above the chest—had passed on to those two vases standing on the chest itself—genuine powder blue—and—no—yes—but something else had been standing there between them—a flash of recollection—there it was—a small oblong ebony box—might have been used for cigarettes—and the box was no longer there. Was there anything in this? Anyhow it was worth noting.

Leaving the house, he made his way back to the pool, filling and lighting his pipe as he did so. The rain was not falling quite so heavily now. He trod warily when he reached the body, knowing that nothing ought to be disturbed before the police came. For this reason, though his curiosity was greatly aroused, he hesitated about any further movement, but tried to take in everything he could see from where he stood.

A few cigarette ends and struck matches were lying about on the path. But they probably meant nothing. Most of the male guests—and several of the other sex—had smoked cigarettes as they walked about the grounds that afternoon. He looked around again. On the farther side of the upper pool, not the one in which the body had been found, but that which was nearly level with the path, was a tiny white patch lying on the ground—about five or six yards from where he was standing.

Now the other side of this upper pool had no path near its edge. Rough undergrowth, nettles, and so forth, extended on either side of a tree trunk. It was quite unlikely that any of the guests at the garden party, clothed as they were in the "glad rags" of a society function, would have wandered over there. What was the white thing he could see?

There was a way of finding out without disturbing matters. As has been said, around this upper pool was a border of rocks with water plants growing in between them. He could use those rocks as stepping stones—for they could bear no footprints. Hastily, stepping from stone to stone, he reached the spot. The little white patch proved to be an oblong bit of tissue paper, lying on a bit of ground that was quite sheltered from the rain. He picked it up.

A cigarette paper. Who had he seen making a cigarette that afternoon? Ah, young Harvey Quarrendau! He had noticed him rolling and licking it. *Licking* it! But this particular paper which was quite dry had no gummed edge on it. It was a foreign variety, such as Spaniards use. They tuck in the ends instead of fastening the edge. He put it back in its place—he wanted to see if the police would notice it—and looked carefully from the rock on which he was standing at the edges of the bank. Just above, the nettles and undergrowth were slightly beaten down. Someone had been standing there.

He came back to the body and tried to reconstruct the crime mentally. For some reason or other the bandsman with the beard had probably followed Nayland—or Nayland had followed the bandsman. Which was it? And why? One of them had hidden on the further side of the pool—ah—that must have been the bandsman, of course. He had never known Nayland smoked anything but cigars. Nayland, then, had probably been standing on the path between the two pools and the bandsman had crept up behind him—probably coming round over those very stones he had just crossed—his crepe soled shoes would make no noise, and had suddenly stabbed Nayland in the back.

Only, there was a flaw in the chain of reasoning. Nayland had been stabbed *through the green jacket*. It was not likely that the murderer had killed him first, withdrawn the knife, changed jackets with the dead man, and then replaced the knife through the green jacket into the same wound. Nayland must have put on the jacket before he was stabbed. Yes, but *why*?

A sudden thought struck him. Perhaps there were two wounds, one which killed Nayland, and the other driven in after the change was made to make it appear that he was wearing the green jacket first. But, again, *why*? Anyhow, the police surgeon—he knew that Major Challow was summoning him over with the rest—would soon settle this point.

And, at this moment, a solemn figure came stalking along the grass path which led from the house, Froome, the local constable. He saluted the Vicar gravely, and immediately produced note book and pencil, moistening the latter with his lips before he began to write. Froome knew the routine that was required of him.

"A bad business this, sir," remarked Froome, shaking his head and making an entry in his book noting the time.

"Very," replied the Vicar.

"But we'll get him, never fear," the policeman went on oracularly, "he can't have got far from what the Major tells me—

how came Mr Nayland to be wearing that smart looking jacket then, sir?" he asked, as for the first time he took in the details.

"That's a question we shall find it difficult to answer," replied Westerham, drily.

"Ah, we'll soon find *that* out," said the other cheerfully, as if dismissing a trifle. "The Major asked the Superintendent to bring Sergeant Ringwood along, and he's a demon for solving things, I tell you, sir—Here they come, I'm thinking."

For the sound of a car was heard, drawing up at "The Pleasaunce," and in a minute or so the Chief Constable appeared, with three others, the Superintendent of the Police at Sydbury, Detective Sergeant Ringwood, and Doctor Thorne—who occupied the post of police surgeon.

The latter made a hasty survey of the body, and shook his head.

"Not much doubt about death being instantaneous," he remarked, "Whoever drove that knife into him knew his business pretty well. We'd best get him indoors now, and then I'll make a further examination."

"You'll be careful of that knife handle, sir," said Ringwood, speaking for the first time, "there may be finger prints."

The doctor hesitated a moment—then said,

"There's nothing to be gained by leaving it in—I can pull it out now."

And did so, taking care to force it upwards by getting his finger under the guard. It was a nasty looking weapon, the blade being about eight inches in length.

"Foreign," muttered the detective as he carefully put it away in a small bag which he had brought, isolating the handle. Westerham glanced at him curiously. He was by no means the ideal of the detective of fiction—rather a burly man, dressed in plain clothes, with a round, chubby face, mild blue eyes, and bristling little fair toothbrush moustache. More childlike humour than intelligence seemed to show on his cheerful, open countenance, and he was very slow and deliberate in his movements.

"I've promised to be with Miss Nayland when she is allowed to see her brother," said the Vicar as the gardener and another man came along with an improvised stretcher to carry the body to the house.

"That won't be for another half hour, I'm afraid," replied the doctor.

"Then is there any objection to my remaining here meanwhile?" asked Westerham, glancing towards Ringwood. The Superintendent also glanced in his direction, raising his eyebrows as if to imply that the decision rested with the detective. The latter turned to the Chief Constable, and said,

"Is this the gentleman that noted what the man we're after was wearing, sir?"

Major Challow nodded.

"Then you may stay, sir, if you like," the detective went on, turning to Westerham. "But if I ask you to go presently you mustn't mind. I like, as a rule, to work alone."

"Ringwood has taken a fancy to that parson, sir," remarked the Superintendent to Major Challow as they turned to go, "I've never known him let an outsider be near him when he's making his notes—you see, he wouldn't even let Froome stay just now."

For Ringwood had curtly dismissed the policeman, for the time being, much to the latter's disappointment.

But even if the detective was willing to allow Westerham to remain with him he did not seem disposed to be communicative. The Vicar, hardened smoker as he was, lighted a fresh pipe and watched him. For several minutes Ringwood stood on the same spot—just above the pool where the murdered man was found —and, slowly turning round, surveyed the scene of the tragedy. Presently Westerham smiled slightly—he saw that Ringwood's eye had caught sight of the cigarette paper. Then he moved for the first time, just as Westerham had done, went to the further side of the pool, picked up the paper, looked at it and put it in his pocket book. But he went further than Westerham, stepped to the bank, seemed to note the slight breaking down of the nettles, went behind the tree trunk and stooped down over a soaking wet patch of thin grass. The Vicar, moving slightly, saw him take a measuring rule from his pocket, apply it to the ground, and make entries in his note book. Then at last, looking up, he spoke.

"Are you sure that bandsman was wearing crepe soled shoes?" he asked.

"Certain."

"Umph!"

Westerham's curiosity was aroused.

"Have you found his footprint?" he asked. "It occurred to me just now he might have been watching Nayland from behind that tree."

"Well, he wasn't," retorted Ringwood, "there *is* a footprint—made after the rain began to fall, too—but it's a clean cut leather sole. What made you think anyone was behind that tree?"

And he looked at the clergyman sharply.

"Observation," replied Westerham.

"Sharp, ain't you?" said the other, coming back to him, "perhaps you observed if anyone this afternoon made their own cigarettes?"

"Not with ungummed papers," retorted the Vicar.

A glint of appreciation showed itself in Ringwood's eyes.

"So you went and had a look at it, eh?" he said, glancing down at the Vicar's feet, "I hope you haven't been trampling the place about."

"You needn't look at my boots," replied Westerham, "I didn't make the footprint over there. I was careful not to walk on anything but those stones."

The glint of admiration expanded into a broad smile.

"You ought to have been one of us, sir," he said, paying the other a genuine compliment. "As it is, I may be glad of your help. What puzzles me is not the tracking of this bandsman—we're seeing to that, of course, and all our stations and the railway booking offices have been warned—but what he and Mr Nayland were doing about that green jacket. I want to re-construct the crime, if it's possible. We've not only got to catch the beggar, but we've got to get sufficient evidence to prove he did it—and some such evidence ought to be here," and he waved his hand.

"There were a lot of people about here this afternoon?" he went on.

"Yes. But not after it was raining."

"I see. Now, tell me please, where does this path lead to?"

And he indicated the continuation of the grassy walk beyond the pools."

"Right through the wood, for three or four hundred yards. Then it comes out into a by-road—at the back of my Vicarage."

The detective nodded.

"I expect it's too sheltered by the trees to get the grass wet enough for impressions," he muttered, half to himself, "but we'll see. Yes. What is it?"

It was Froome who had arrived to say that Dr Thorne had finished his examination and would the Vicar come? The detective called the policeman to him before the latter followed Westerham back to the house.

"I want you to bring me one of Mr Nayland's boots that he was wearing—the right one."

Left to himself Ringwood seemed to become more alert; quicker in his movements. It was part of his stock in trade never, if he could help it, to let others see into the whole of his character and temperament. Rapidly he moved from place to place around, and chiefly beyond the scene of the crime, using his eyes keenly as he did so. When Froome came back with the boot he relapsed for a minute into his lethargic movements, but was very soon at work again. He measured the sole of the boot, went to the further side of the pool and stooped over the ground with it, examined certain marks on the grassy path leading beyond the pools, and then disappeared along it—entering the wood.

Twenty minutes later he had returned to "The Pleasaunce" and had joined the Chief Constable and the superintendent in the library. At his particular request the Vicar was also present, but the Doctor had gone. The detective asked for his report.

"Just what we expected," said the Superintendent, "stabbed through the heart from behind. Death instantaneous."

"More than one wound?" asked Westerham.

"Why, no. One was enough, I should think," said Major Challow, in a tone of surprise.

But the detective nodded towards the Vicar approvingly.

"Ah!" he said, "that makes it certain that he was wearing the green jacket before he was stabbed. I wonder why?"

"May we ask if you have discovered anything, Ringwood?" questioned the Major. He knew his man, and was not prepared to force his hand.

"Well," said the detective, "as far as it's gone it looks like a very simple case—I mean as to the facts. We may find out more about a motive when we get to know something about Mr Nayland himself—if we can. But there isn't any doubt that he was killed by the bandsman, though I confess I'm fairly puzzled about that jacket. From what I've been able to make out it looks as though Mr Nayland was, at one time, standing behind a tree by one of the pools—his footprint's there—Yes, sir," he added, turning to the Vicar, "there's little doubt about that. And this bandsman was probably with him there, though, because he was wearing crepe soled shoes I can't trace his footprints. But I found, close by, a foreign cigarette paper, and Mr Westerham tells me Nayland did not smoke cigarettes. That points to the conclusion that someone was with him there. Nayland seems to have walked up and down once or twice on the path between the pools. Beyond that it's practically impossible to trace footsteps, the ground is too dry under the trees, but when I got on to the road the other side of the wood there's positive proof that the murderer went along it—the print of his crepe soled shoes is as plain as a pikestaff in the fresh mud. Also, I've found something. Look here!"

He opened his little bag and produced a false black beard, fixed on wire.

"Gad!" exclaimed Major Challow, "that was it—was it? Pity we sent out his description as wearing a beard."

Ringwood smiled.

"I'd thought of that, sir, before I came. A man with a big beard is always suspicious. So I had suggested that the description might imply that he was with or without it. There's something else, though."

Diving into his bag again he produced a number of bits of wood—dead black in colour, and splintered. Westerham leaned forward eagerly.

"Where did you find those?" he asked.

"Halfway through the wood—on the side of the path. There are one or two biggish stones lying about there, and one of these had evidently been used to smash what looks like some kind of a box. I don't know that there is anything in it, though."

"But there is," exclaimed Westerham, "I recognise the moulding. It was an ebony box that stood on a chest in the hall—and that bandsman must have taken it."

And he told them how he had missed it.

"Robbery—and then murder," said the detective. "Looks like it, anyway. Well, sir," he went on to the Chief Constable, "we've got to find out who this bandsman was. Miss Nayland will be able to tell us where the Band was engaged, and I'll run up to London and get some news there."

"He left his overcoat and violin, whoever he was," broke in Westerham, "they might form a clue."

"Good! I'll look at them presently. I should like to ask Miss Nayland a few questions—if she's up to it—and the servants. Oh, there's just one more thing—"

And he opened his bag again, looked inside, hesitated, shook his head, closed the bag with a snap, and asked abruptly,

"Anyone know of any person likely to have been here this afternoon whose initials are D.G.?"

"D.G.?" said Major Challow, "Gad—yes! One of the guests—but quite out of the question, Ringwood. Miss Garforth. Her Christian name is Diana."

"But—!" ejaculated the Vicar, colouring as he did so, "Why—what?"

But the detective smiled at him.

"It's nothing sir.—Well—I'd like to question these people by themselves."

CHAPTER 3

Major Challow and the Superintendent had returned to Sydbury. Westerham had gone back to his Vicarage. Detective Sergeant Ringwood sat in the library alone, jotting down one or two notes in his book. As he had said, to him the actual crime and the extreme possibility of laying hands on the perpetrator, who could have hardly covered up his tracks in so short a time, presented no particular difficulty. But there were certain things he wanted to know, certain data which would have to be pieced together to construct the case when the time came, and there was also—in spite of the plain facts—a decided mystery about the whole affair which baffled him. So he had sent word to Miss Nayland to ask if she could see him for a few minutes.

Presently she came into the library herself. He could see at once that she was not a demonstrative person; her quiet, self-possessed attitude told him that; but, at the same time, he noticed the paleness of her cheeks and the redness of her eyes, and he knew that she was feeling the tragedy acutely.

He rose from his seat and bowed. She had really dreaded being confronted with a policeman and only a stern sense of duty had made her consent to see him. But his genuine air of sympathy and his pleasant, almost childlike face, re-assured her.

"I am so sorry," he began, "to trouble you—and if you had rather not I can easily wait till some other time—"

"No," she interrupted him, "I know you must want to see me—and I will give you any help I can."

"Thank you so much, Miss Nayland. I will be as brief as possible. But there are a few simple questions I should like to ask you. In the first place can you tell me where the Band was engaged?"

"Yes—from an agency. 'The Apollo Concert Direction', Old Bond Street—I forget the number."

The detective nodded.

"Don't trouble," he said, "I can easily find that out. Did you notice this man with the beard this afternoon?"

"I remember him slightly."

"You had never seen him before?"

"Not that I know of."

"I suppose your brother said nothing to you about him?"

"Oh, no. As a matter of fact I hardly spoke to my brother all the afternoon."

"Tell me, Miss Nayland, your brother had been abroad a good deal hadn't he?"

"Oh yes. He was a great traveller. He only settled down here last autumn. For six or seven years we had not met."

"Was he abroad all that time?"

"Yes."

"And where?"

"Oh, all sorts of places. He was on an expedition in Central Asia. Also he went to Corea. For the last three years—before he came home—he was in South America."

The detective nodded thoughtfully.

"I see—yes. I suppose it would be possible to find out what he was doing there? Perhaps you could tell me?"

She shook her head.

"Not very much. My brother was rather a reticent man. He never spoke much about his travels—not even to me. Sometimes, but very rarely, people used to come and see him—I mean people he had met abroad."

"Could you tell me anything about them?"

"I'm afraid I can't."

"Were any of them foreigners?"

She thought for a moment.

"Ye-es—at least I remember one who was—he spoke very little

English. My brother talked to him in Spanish."

"What was his name?"

"Oh—let me see—Valdez, I think—or something like that."

"I see. And now, can you tell me anything about this?" and he showed her the broken fragments of the ebony box. "Mr Westerham says it stood in the hall."

"Of course it did. How did it get broken?"

He told her.

"Do you know anything about it?"

"Why, it is curious," she replied, "but this very man—Valdez—brought it with him when he came. I remember now. He gave it to him just as he was leaving; he spoke of it as being a memento of something, and suggested that my brother might like to add it to his collection. It has stood on one of the Corean chests in the hall ever since."

"How long ago was this?"

"Oh, it was sometime in June."

"Did you keep it locked?"

"Oh, dear no. I don't know that there *was* a lock to it—certainly no key. I used it to keep odd packets of flower seeds in."

The detective smiled, and looked in his bag.

"Yes," he said, "I found some little packets of seeds scattered about among the fragments of the box. Queer! For it was evidently this box that the fellow was after. Are you sure there was nothing else in it?"

"Positively certain. It was quite empty when my brother first had it."

"Umph! Well, I'm very grateful to you Miss Nayland. As a matter of form I shall have to see the servants. There's nothing suspicious about them, I suppose?"

"Oh dear no. Not that I know of. Oh, there is one thing I thought you might like to have," and she produced a paper, "I kept a list of all the guests we invited for this afternoon, with a cross against those who accepted."

"Thank you very much," he said, as he took the paper, "but I don't suppose I shall want it. All we have to do is to get hold of this bandsman—and I think we shall."

"I hope you will—it is all so very terrible—I can't realise it yet."

"Of course," he said, soothingly, "I quite understand. You have my sympathy, Miss Nayland. Thank you so much."

"Do you wish to stay here?" she asked, her hand on the door handle, "anything I can do—"

"No, no. I'm going back to Sydbury as soon as I have seen the servants."

"Then let me send you in some refreshment."

"It is very kind of you."

When she had gone he made a move towards the bell, and then hesitated.

"No," he said to himself, "I'll see who comes first—it's a more natural way."

In five minutes time the butler came in, carrying a tray on which were sandwiches and biscuits—the former probably the remains of the afternoon refreshments—and a whisky decanter and syphon. He put them down on a table near the detective.

"Is there anything else you'd like?" he asked, and Ringwood noticed he omitted the "sir." Well, he was only a policeman.

"That will do me all right," he said, "don't go," for the man was preparing to leave the room, "I'd like a bit of a chat if you've got a few minutes. This is a horrible affair, and you may help me."

He spoke in an easy, familiar tone, helping himself to a sandwich as he did so.

"Yes?" said the butler, expectantly.

"Oh, sit down, won't you. That's better. I expect you're a bit upset, eh?"

"I am," replied the butler, emphatically, "I've lost a good master —and it's a bad shock to me."

"How long have you been with him?"

"Ever since he came home from abroad."

"Oh—he engaged you then, did he?"

"Not exactly. He engaged me on the way home. I was steward on board the 'Pelican,' one of the Blue Diamond liners, and Miss Nayland came back from Rio in her. His stateroom was on my deck and I suppose I suited him, for he said he'd make it worth my while if I gave up the job and came to him. So I did."

The detective took a sip from his tumbler and glanced over it keenly at the other. The butler, a model of quiet decorum, had an easy manner and was evidently willing to talk.

"I see. By the way, what's your name?"

"Burt—James Burt."

"Well, I'm sorry you've lost such a good master. Now, tell me, you've been about all the afternoon, I suppose?"

"Yes, of course. There was a good deal to see to."

"Naturally. And you noticed this bandsman—the one with the black beard?"

"In a way, yes. The fact of his having a beard, you see—"

"Exactly. Now, when did you first notice him?"

Burt thought for a moment.

"I think it was when the Band came to have their tea—in the marquee."

"What time was that?"

"Between half past five and six—after the guests had finished."

Ringwood consulted his note book.

"But," he said sharply, "this particular man does not appear to have stayed with the rest all the time they were having tea, eh?"

"That is so," replied Burt.

"Did you see him afterwards?"

"Yes."

"Where?"

For a moment or two Burt appeared to be making an effort to recollect. Then he said,

"I'll tell you all I saw—though it wasn't much. I was in the marquee when the concert was going on in the hall. I could just see the terrace in front of the house from where I was standing. The bandsman with the beard came out, and stood for a minute or two on the terrace—there was a little crowd of people there all the time. All of a sudden he stepped on to the lawn, but just at that moment Mr Nayland came out, looked round about him, saw the bandsman and followed him—just as he seemed to be

33

making for the garden."

"Did he overtake him?"

"Yes when he was crossing the paddock."

"Did you hear what they said?"

"No, I was too far away."

"Is that all you saw?"

"That's all I saw, Mr Ringwood."

"He left his overcoat and violin, didn't he?"

"Yes. They're in the small room which the Band and the Glee Singers used for dressing."

"Well, bring them along here to me, please. And then you can tell the servants I want to see them, one by one. Don't frighten them."

"Very good."

When Burt had brought in the overcoat and violin, Ringwood examined them rapidly. The coat was an ordinary fawn raincoat, with the maker's name on the collar tab. The detective turned out the pockets, but found only a silk neck handkerchief and an early edition of a London evening paper. Nothing more.

He questioned the other servants cursorily, but there was nothing to be found in that quarter. Then he asked if he could be run into Sydbury, and, while waiting for the car, sauntered out on the lawn and went into the marquee. There was no one there. The hired crockery had been packed into boxes, and there was a litter of paper, crumbs, and so on about the ground. One thing attracted his attention—a cigarette end. He picked it up. Yes, it was a hand rolled one, and there was no gum on the paper. He put it away carefully in his little bag.

It was quite late in the evening when Ringwood arrived at Sydbury, and darkness was setting in. His first action was to go to the police station and enquire as to whether anything had been heard of the missing bandsman. But the Superintendent shook his head.

"It's queer," he said, "but there's not a vestige of a report from any quarter. Unless he got someone to motor him in to Sydbury he could hardly have got here before we were warned about him.

You remember we got the phone message from Major Challow just before half past six and sent Blake to the station here immediately. The first train out was a bit late—the one timed to reach Coppleswick at 6.45. He wasn't on that, and it wasn't likely he would be. And every train since has been watched. How about that 6.45 up from Coppleswick?"

"I went to the station and enquired of the station master about that," replied Ringwood. "It was the train by which the Band went back to London. It's only a small station, as you know, and the station master said that beside the Band there were just three other passengers—whom he knew. As a matter of fact the Bandmaster spoke to him about this missing fellow and asked him to tell him if he *should* turn up by the next train to hurry to some engagement they had in London. So the station master was on the look out for him before we phoned. No, he didn't make his getaway there."

Ringwood went on to describe his investigations so far as they centred upon the mysterious bandsman.

"I'll run up to London by the first train tomorrow and enquire of this agency," he said, "we shall probably find his address. Meanwhile everything points to his being a foreigner— with some connection with Nayland mixed up with his travels abroad. The motive probably lies there. I shall look in at Scotland Yard. I want a list of any South American suspects known to be in this country. The fact that he carried a knife and smoked a Spanish form of cigarette is all on a level with what Miss Nayland told me about her brother having lived three years in South America before he came home."

He carried out his resolution the next morning, and the first place he visited was the Apollo Concert Direction in Old Bond Street. Here he asked to see the manager, explained who he was, and requested information about the Green Albanian Band.

"It's a private Band," explained the manager, "we only act as agents, you see. We don't know any of the individual members of it, but of course the Bandmaster can tell you. I'll look up his name and address—ah—here it is—Broadwater's the man you want—he lives at 13, Mayfield Road, Hampstead."

A taxi soon carried the detective to Mayfield Road. Broadwater was at home.

"I thought the police would be here pretty soon," he said, "I've just read about the murder in this morning's paper—in fact I was just asking myself whether I ought not to communicate with Scotland Yard when you came in."

"I'm glad for some things you didn't," said the detective, "we haven't called the Yard into the case yet and I hope we shan't have to. We're a bit on our own mettle, you see. Now, tell me, what was the name of this fellow?"

"I don't know, I never set eyes on him till yesterday."

"But surely, he's a member of your Band?"

"No he isn't. That's just the point. He came as a substitute—for our second violinist."

"But how?"

"Well, our rule is that if one of us is unable to fulfil an engagement through illness or anything that he has to provide a substitute. It's a very usual thing. Anstey, that's the second violinist—phoned me yesterday morning that he couldn't run down to Coppleswick, but would provide a man who would play in his place—said he'd meet us at the station, and he did."

"His name?"

"Upon my word, I forget. But Anstey will tell you that. Shall I ring him up?"

"If you would. Tell him I'll go and see him at once."

"He lives quite close—in the Abbey Road," explained Broadwater as he waited for the exchange to put him on . . . "Yes—hullo?—Is that you, Anstey?—right—There's a detective coming to see you about this Coppleswick business—yes—*now*, at once . . . What's that? Yes? . . . Well, you must tell him all you can—that's all."

"Seems in no end of a funk about it," he added, as he hung up the receiver, "he's a nervous chap, is Anstey, and this has upset him a lot apparently. What a horrible business the whole affair is. Do you think it likely—"

"Excuse my interrupting you," broke in Ringwood, "but my time's precious, and I want to ask you a few questions before I go. Now, when did you first see this fellow we're after?"

"At the station—Marylebone—when we started. He came up and introduced himself as Anstey's substitute."

"What did you say?"

"I asked him if he knew the music, of course, and he said he did. Anstey had given him the programme."

"Anything else?"

"Yes—about our uniform. Anstey had lent him his jacket and he was wearing it under his rain coat."

"Did you notice anything particular about him on the journey down?"

"Only that he was evidently a foreigner. He was a silent sort of man, and was reading a paper most of the way."

"Did he play correctly when you were at Coppleswick?"

"Oh, yes—fairly well. I thought him a bit of an amateur at the time. He was not up to our general level."

"Yes. And what happened? Did you notice his movements?"

"Only that I missed him after we'd finished. He had some tea with the rest of us in the marquee, but went out when we were in the middle of ours. I never saw him afterwards."

"Didn't ask you any questions—about the place—or Nayland?"

"Oh, no. As a matter of fact he hardly spoke at all."

"Thanks. I think that's all."

And, refusing to stay any longer, in spite of the Bandmaster's evident desire to discuss the murder, he made for the taxi, which was waiting for him outside, and drove straight off to the address in the Abbey Road.

Broadwater was quite correct when he said that Anstey was afflicted with nerves. He was a little, stout man, with rather long, fair hair, and a drooping moustache, a pale, refined face and restless eyes, the long fingers on his hands continuously moving restlessly as he spoke.

"I'm very glad to see you," he exclaimed to the detective, "ever since I opened my paper this morning I've scarcely known what to do. Tell me, shall I have to give evidence? Do you think I shall be arrested? If I'd had the slightest idea of what was going to happen—but how could I know? You can see it wasn't my fault, I hope?"

He was walking up and down the room as he talked. The detective assumed a soothing attitude.

"Please don't be alarmed, Mr Anstey. And would you object to my smoking?"

The other rushed for a box of cigarettes that stood on the mantlepiece and offered it to Ringwood.

"Of course. Please take one. You see, I had no idea—"

"Won't you smoke yourself, Mr Anstey?"

"Oh—yes. But, you see—"

"Now, please don't worry," said the detective, quietly, as Anstey threw himself into a chair. "Mr Broadwater has told me you did a very ordinary thing in engaging a substitute to play for you at Coppleswick yesterday. Well, there's no harm in that. All I've come here for is to find out what you can tell me about this substitute. I want you to help us."

"Of course I will if I can. But you don't think anyone suspects —"

"Now, look here, Mr Anstey. You mustn't imagine that because I'm a policeman I've got anything against you. I haven't. Try to tell me just what happened. Begin at the beginning, and tell me in your own way."

For he saw that a series of questions would only confuse this nervous little man. Half closing his eyes, and puffing away quietly at his cigarette, he listened while Anstey told his story, told it a little incoherently, perhaps, but the detective pieced it together without interrupting.

"It was the day before yesterday he called here. I'd never seen him before, and wondered what he wanted. He said his name was Lenoir—of course I saw he was a foreigner—as soon as he spoke—and that he played first violin in a Parisian orchestra and was also an author. He was on a visit to England, he told me, and wanted to write some articles on English social life. He had heard that the Green Albanian Band was going to play at a garden party given by a great nobleman—of course I told him he *wasn't* a nobleman at all, but he said it made no difference. He wanted to see what an English garden party at a big country house was like and would I allow him to take my place? Of course he would pay me—and then—and then, you see, he offered me ten pounds. I—I—am not very well off, you know, and it was a natural temptation—and I didn't see how there could be any harm in it. I told him he would have to wear the uniform—it's a green coat, you know—and, in the end, he paid me the ten pounds then and there, and I let him take the coat away—oh, yes —but I told him we had another engagement after the garden party—last night—and he said I could meet him up here—at the station—when the Band returned—he would leave his bag with his own coat in it at the cloak room—and we could change in the waiting room. Of course I went to the station last night and met the Band, but he wasn't there. I had to play in my ordinary coat— Broadwater was a bit put out about it, but it wasn't my fault."

The detective looked up.

"I wish we could spot that bag," he said, "It might be useful."

"He had it with him."

"Here?"

"Yes—he put the green coat in it—it may not have been the same bag, of course, but anyhow he had one."

"Can you describe it?"

"A small light brown bag—the shape I think they call a gladstone. I noticed it because a patch of the leather was stained on one side—it looked as if some ink had been spilt on it. Do you think I shall get my uniform jacket back? We have to buy our own, you see, and they're expensive."

The detective smiled a little grimly as he thought of that jacket. The fact that Nayland had been wearing it when he was murdered had not come out in the brief press report.

"Yes—you'll get it again," he said, "but I'm afraid you'll find it a bit damaged. It's had a soaking in water—and it's torn," he added grimly.

"How did it get torn?"

"You'll find out later on. Now it's queer," he went on, half speaking to himself, "Either he was lying and didn't mean to put that bag in the cloak room at all, or else he must be a confoundedly cool hand. He goes down to Coppleswick with the evident intention of getting Nayland apart and sticking a knife into him, and calmly arranges to travel back with the Band afterwards and give up the green jacket to you. And yet," and he frowned thoughtfully, "that doesn't fit in with what really happened. And there's always the difficulty of Nayland wearing the thing . . . . . Thank you very much for all you've told me, Mr Anstey. One thing more. Did he give you his address by any chance?"

Anstey shook his head.

"Oh, no. He never mentioned it."

"Very well. I think that's all you can tell me."

The little man got up.

"And you don't blame me? You don't think—"

"Look here" broke in Ringwood soothingly, "You've nothing to be afraid of at all. You will have to give evidence at the inquest, and when we catch this beggar—which ought to be soon—of course you'll be wanted as a witness for the prosecution. But yours is a perfectly plain story. You've done nothing in any way wrong, and you won't be affected by it. Only you must expect that the newspaper fellows will try to interview you when they get hold of more details. That's only natural."

"I shall keep away from them," replied the little man as he shook hands with Ringwood. "Thank you very much for coming. You've relieved me immensely."

"There's only one thing more," said the detective, pausing at the door, "should you recognise this man if you saw him?"

"I should know him by his beard."

"He's taken that off. Anything else?"

"Ye-es, I think so. He had remarkably dark eyes—and thick bushy eyebrows. And I should know his voice."

"Well, if you do come across him by any chance, make straight for the nearest policeman—not that you're likely to. Good morning, Mr Anstey, and thank you once more."

CHAPTER 4

Re-entering his taxi once more Ringwood drove to Marylebone Station, the terminus of the line from Sydbury. He had very little hope of finding the bag that Anstey had mentioned, as he did not believe for an instant that it had been deposited there, but he felt it a part of his duty to make enquiries nevertheless.

Marylebone is the quietest of the great London Termini, and its cloak room is quite small in comparison with the others. Seeking an Inspector in his office the detective explained his errand, and the two men made their way into the cloak room.

"You can have a look round, at all events," he said, "Here, Babeson," he went on to the clerk in charge, "you can answer any questions this gentleman asks you."

"Yes, sir?" said the clerk.

"I suppose you couldn't tell me whether you noticed a man who was wearing a green jacket under a fawn raincoat, who is said to have left a small brown bag here yesterday?"

The clerk shook his head.

"No, I couldn't," he replied, "do you know about what time it was?"

"Not exactly—but before the 2.10 stopping train to Sydbury."

"Yes, I was here on duty up till then. It would be somewhere around here," and he pointed out a division of the racks surrounding the room, "unless it's been taken out."

There were several small brown bags on the rack. And one of them had what looked like a splash of ink on its side. The clerk looked at the counterfoil label.

"Yes," he said, "this was put in some time after mid-day

yesterday. I can tell that by the number."

The detective took it down from the rack and pressed the spring fastening. It was not locked, and opened at once. The contents consisted of a jacket of some nondescript, dark material, and a clean pocket handkerchief. Nothing more.

Eagerly the detective examined the pockets of the jacket, but gave a grunt of disappointment. They were empty. Then he turned to the handkerchief. There was a little more information here. It was marked with the initials "M.G."

"Now, look here," he said to the Inspector, as he put the jacket and handkerchief back into the bag, "I don't expect for a moment he'll be such a fool as to try to get this out. But anyone who *does* give in the voucher must be detained."

"Certainly," replied the Inspector, "we'll arrange that all right."

Once more Ringwood got into his taxi, telling the driver to take him to Scotland Yard. But he was sorely puzzled. If this elusive bandsman had gone to Coppleswick with the deliberate intention of murdering Felix Nayland, why had he made these elaborate arrangements to change his coat at Marylebone when he got back? The evidence that he was the murderer was perfectly clear. The only solution seemed to be that his original plan had miscarried, that he must have taken a sudden fright after committing the crime. And then, there was always the bewildering question, "Why was Felix Nayland wearing that jacket?" It was an unheard of thing in the annals of crime for a murderer to change clothes with his victim in such a bizarre manner. Why did the change take place? If the murderer intended, as he appeared to have done, to give Anstey back his uniform, and had made preparations for doing so, how on earth was it that he managed to get this conspicuous garment on Nayland? And—always—why?

It was with these thoughts in his mind that he reached Scotland Yard. Explaining his errand to an official he was quickly shown into a room, where he was greeted by a genial Inspector in plain clothes.

"Ah," said the latter, "I'm not surprised to see you. It's about this Coppleswick case I suppose, eh? Haven't laid hands on the fellow yet?"

"No—but we ought to, I think."

"Yes," said the other, nodding gravely, "you ought to. From what I hear you must have had the luck to be on the spot almost immediately after the murder?"

"We were."

"And yet—no trace, eh?"

"Oh, I won't say that, sir. Our men are at work down there. He can't have got far."

The Inspector looked at him curiously—with a little smile.

"Thinking of calling us in?" he asked.

"That's not for me to say, sir. I've come up now for some information. That's all."

"I see. Well, fire away."

The detective briefly explained matters.

"You see," he added, "the fact that the man was evidently a foreigner, carried a knife, smoked a Spanish form of cigarette, (for Nayland did not smoke cigarettes), coupled with the fact that Nayland has recently been three years in South America, seems to point to several things—probably to the motive among others. What I want to get at is any suspicious characters from South America who happen to be in this country just now. I suppose you have them?"

"Yes," said the other, drily, "we have them," and he glanced at a file cabinet which stood on the table. "That's my particular department."

He unlocked the cabinet and took out some files. They were labelled respectively "Political," "Communist," "Confidence men," and so forth.

"As a matter of fact," he said, "our South American friends don't make a big list in this country. The United States are generally their refuge—or over the Mexican border. Now this particular case doesn't seem to be associated with the ordinary crook—"

"How about the robbery of that ebony box, though?" broke in

Ringwood.

"Um, yes. There's that, of course. Might have contained valuables—jewels, for example, in a secret cavity, which would account for smashing it. Found out anything about its history?"

"Yes. Miss Nayland—the dead man's sister—says it was given to her brother by a man named Valdez, who stayed there a time ago."

"Oh! Valdez—Valdez," and he repeated the name as he ran his finger over the index of each file, "That doesn't seem to help us much—no—there's no such name or alias here. But it's important, of course—you can see that?"

"Certainly. It's a clue to the motive. Look here, sir; I figure it out like this. Provided Nayland himself is clear of any suspicion—"

"You don't know," interrupted the other, sharply, "you can't tell at this stage what Nayland might or might not have been up to when he was abroad. But go on—yes—provided Nayland was all right?"

"Well, in that case, as Valdez was a friend of his, he isn't likely to be a crook, is he?"

"There may be something in that—yes. But there's always the other alternative. Anyhow I'll make a note of it and if I can find out anything of this Valdez I'll let you know. Now, this fellow you're after. He may be clean shaven or he may have had a genuine moustache under his false beard. There's not much to go upon."

"His initials on the handkerchief I found this morning, 'M.G.'"

"Ah—" again he ran his finger down the lists, "No, we're at sea again there. Well, now, take this Communist lot—there are only three of them in the country now, small fry. And I fancy they are up north. Half a minute."

He took up the telephone and made some enquiries—to another department.

"Yes—they're all in Glasgow—in the strike business there. Under observation, of course. Now take the politicals."

Photographs, with accompanying memoranda, were discussed briefly.

"That's old de Soto—quite a harmless old boy. President of Santa Fedora for exactly three weeks, years ago, and been scheming to get back ever since. Here's Pedro Fernandez, mixed up in some shady political move in Guatemala—as big a coward and skunk as you make 'em. He's not likely to be your man. This is a chap of entirely different calibre. Rejoices in the name of Patrick Maria O'Calligan."

"Irish?"

"His father was—married a South American girl. O'Calligan's a half breed. Deucedly clever chap. Speaks English without an accent and Spanish like a Spaniard. A very dangerous fellow, a political adventurer of the worst type. He wouldn't stop short of murder—and hasn't either. Ever heard of the insurrection last year in San Miguel—a potty little state north of Brazil? No? He was secretary to Don Gonzolez, the leader of it, and turned traitor afterwards. He's badly wanted out there. There was another blackguard associated with him, an Englishman named Beech—a fair haired scoundrel who got away just in time to save his skin. No one knows what became of him, but there was more than one dago who would have taken his life on sight, and they say there's one fellow whose two sons he killed, who swore to track him down wherever he was. A shady lot, all of 'em—yes, that's O'Calligan."

Ringwood was looking at the portrait of a man with a refined face, delicately arched eyebrows, thin lips, and a dreamy expression in his eyes.

"Doesn't look a rogue, eh?" asked the Inspector. "Yes—that's 'Red O'Calligan,' so called because of the colour of his hair, and his record. He's in London now. But he isn't your man. I happen to know that he couldn't play any musical instrument to save his life. And your man is a musician. Don't forget that!—Well, I'm afraid that's all I can do for you—you don't see anyone likely among this little collection?"

Ringwood shook his head.

"I'd better be getting back to Sydbury," he said, "and see what's doing there. We've got a smart man on the trail, and I hope something's turned up by this time, sir."

"Ah! Good luck to you. And if you should want us," and he laughed, "I expect your Chief will let us know. I know Challow," he added, "and I fancy he'll try to get all the credit. But it's an interesting case—and I shan't forget it!"

"Oh, by the way," he ejaculated, as Ringwood was going out of the room, "that knife! How about finger prints?"

"I'm just going to see one of your experts now, sir," replied Ringwood, "I've brought the knife with me—it was a bit too delicate a matter for us to tackle. You see it had been in the water. That's the worst of it."

"I don't know," replied the Inspector, "Harley—that's our best man here—will make a job of it if it's to be done. Finger prints, you must remember, are really more or less impressions formed by greasy exhumation from the skin pores, and if the handle was simply in the water, and didn't get wiped about, there's a chance of getting something out of it. Grease is inclined to be impervious in cold water, you know. How long was it in the water?"

"Couldn't have been very long, sir. Twenty minutes at the outside, according to my findings. You think there's a chance?"

"There may be. I've known a similar case. Of course it's worth trying. Go and see Harley about it—good day."

*

Ringwood got out at Coppleswick Station on his way back to Sydbury, having previously arranged with Holt, a capable young officer he had placed on the job, to meet him there. But Holt shook his head, sadly.

"Not a trace, Sergeant," he said, "and there isn't a stone we've left unturned. I've been in every house in Coppleswick and seen practically everyone there is in the village. No one could give me any information. The whole countryside has been raked through. How he got away is a mystery."

"And we've got to solve that mystery," said the detective

grimly, "only one out of two things can have happened. Either he managed to get clear away, or he's still in the neighbourhood. We've got to find him, somehow, and I mean to do it if it's to be done at all. I suppose there are plenty of press representatives about?"

"The place swarms with 'em, Sergeant. They've pestered me whenever they could get hold of me."

"I daresay. Any of them staying in the village?"

"Two, I think, at the 'Red Lion': the 'Daily Eagle' and the 'Evening Gazette' men."

"All right. Get hold of them, will you, and tell them I'll meet them at the 'Red Lion' in an hour's time. You can say I've got special information for them. I've a call to pay first. I shall want you after I've seen these pressmen, and then I'll get back to Sydbury."

His call was at the Vicarage. Westerham, who was at home, welcomed him heartily, took him into his study, and gave him a good cigar.

"Any news?" he asked the detective, "that is, if I'm not out of order in enquiring?"

"Not at all," replied Ringwood, "you've given me considerable help, Mr Westerham, and I've no objection to taking you into my confidence—though I'm afraid it isn't much I have to tell you. I've just come down from London, and I've found out that this bandsman was not a member of the band at all. Well, I don't suppose that surprises you?"

Westerham paused in the act of lighting his pipe,

"No," he replied, "I had guessed that already. Have you found out who he is?"

"I can't say I have. He gave the name Lenoir to the violinist whose place he took, but I don't suppose for a moment this is right, and I fancy I've got the initials of his real name—'M.G.', if I'm not mistaken."

The Vicar shot a keen glance at him.

"You don't mean 'D.G.?'" he asked.

"No."

And Westerham noticed his sudden reticence—and made a mental note that the man was keeping something back from him. Then Ringwood proceeded to tell him of the interviews he had had in London, and about the bag in the cloak room, and its contents. But, when he spoke of his visit to Scotland Yard he merely said that nothing had come of it—that there was no South American suspect among the records who seemed to have any connection with the case.

"There, sir," he said, "I've laid my cards on the table. After what I saw of you yesterday may I say I've a respect for your opinion—and I'd like to have it."

The Vicar smoked in silence for a few moments, then gave a little laugh, and said,

"At present it's like Mrs Beeton's cookery book—first catch your hare, you know. But—apart from that—you've got hold of some interesting details. Here's a fellow who makes elaborate arrangements to get down here in an assumed character, ostensibly for the purpose of getting hold of that ebony box. Mind you, we don't *know* that he meant to kill Nayland. It's more than probable that he didn't intend murder, hence the equally elaborate preparations to slip out of his assumed character. You've got to remember that Nayland came across him *accidentally* in the hall, and probably spotted who he was. Following upon that it's much more likely that Nayland was after him than that he was after Nayland. Don't you think so?"

The detective pondered for a moment. Then he said "You mean that afterwards there was a quarrel? That Nayland, say, found he had taken the box and tried to get it back, and that the fellow killed him on the spur of the moment? Is that what you mean, Mr Westerham?"

"That's an inference, isn't it?"

"And your theory, then?"

"Oh no," replied the Vicar, quickly, "don't you go away with the idea that I've got a theory, because, honestly, I haven't. I'm not a crime expert! It's not in my line. Only, as I told Major Challow yesterday, I've made a habit of observing things. And I confess

I'm deeply interested in the affair, not only because I may call Nayland a personal friend, but because I'm a man who always wants to get at the reasons of things. I suppose I've a logical turn of mind. But I want to observe a bit more before I form any theory. The thing may have happened as I suggest. But it doesn't account for Nayland wearing that coat, does it?"

Ringwood brought his hand down on his knee with a resounding slap.

"Oh, hang the coat!"

"What you want to do is to hang the man who wore it," said the Vicar, grimly.

"Well, there's about enough evidence to hang him—when we catch him, isn't there?"

But Westerham did not reply with a ready acquiescence. When he did so, he said slowly, "I suppose there is—from your point of view. But, as I have said, I've not formed any theory. So I won't commit myself. First find your hare, Sergeant. I suppose you've taken all possible steps to do that?"

"Of course we have. All stations are warned, and all ports of embarkation. We've put all the machinery we can into motion. And I'm just going to see a couple of press representatives and tell them certain things I want them to publish."

"Such as?"

"The man's description, so far as we know it. The fact that he was acting as a substitute in the band, the initials 'M.G.' and a request that any hotelkeeper or landlady who has missed a guest or lodger, or who has any foreigner in their house with these initials—and so forth, you know—should communicate with the editors. Editors like to have a share in the game, and they're useful—if you only let 'em know what you want 'em to know."

Westerham laughed.

"You won't mention the bag in the cloak room, for instance?"

"By Gad, no! Not that I think he'll be such a fool as to try to claim it. Do you?"

"I don't know. He may not have seen today's paper yet."

"But what's that to do with it, sir? There's nothing about that bag in the morning editions."

"Quite so," replied the Vicar, "Well, I wish you all success!"

"One thing more. You knew Nayland very well?"

"We were friends," admitted Westerham, "but he was a new parishioner. I never saw him before he came here—in March last."

"But he used to talk to you about his travels?"

"Not very much. I could see he'd had adventures, but he was a reticent man—with an Englishman's hatred of talking about his own best doings."

"Or *worst* doings, perhaps," said the detective.

"Ah, well," replied Westerham, "we mustn't judge the poor chap. But you know there are fellows who consider their worst doings their best—not that I should accuse him of that. He didn't seem the sort of man who would have run crooked. But, as I say, he'd evidently had his innings in out of the way places, and that generally means a story. But if there was one, he never hinted at it to me."

"Do you think there was one?" asked the other, tersely.

"Why, of course I do, man! Just look at the facts. A mysterious empty box. Someone after it. And a murder at the end of it all. Of course there's a story. But you and I will probably never know it."

When the detective had taken his departure the Vicar of Coppleswick refilled his pipe, lighted it, sat down in an arm chair and drew up another one on which to place his feet, a favourite attitude of his when he wanted to think out sermons or parochial problems.

Westerham, to the external world, was an energetic, capable parish priest, a good organizer, and a plain, sensible preacher. Therefore the ordinary external world labelled him as a parson and pigeon-holed him accordingly. Most people have the extraordinary notion that a clergyman is something different from an ordinary man, that he lives entirely apart from others in a theological atmosphere and only looks out on life from a religious standpoint. It is ludicrous, at times, to notice how, in society, the host or hostess will try to talk shop to a parson, the latest utterance of a Bishop, ecclesiastical architecture, Sunday School treats, Mothers' Meetings, when, all the time, they would certainly not attempt to talk to a surgeon about his operations, or to a lawyer about conveyances of leasehold properties. In nine cases out of ten, also, that parson doesn't want to talk shop at all —only, as has been said, they have labelled him and stuffed him into a mental pigeon-hole—and won't let him get out.

Apart from being an energetic parish priest Westerham was a particularly shrewd and capable man. And it was no idle boast of his that he had made a habit of observation—many of his parishioners little guessed how closely and clearly he had summed them up by observing those ordinary idiosyncrasies which escape the notice of most people.

lie was also a man who could be deeply interested in many things quite apart from his professional calling, and chiefly in problems which concerned humanity. And this particular problem had attracted him greatly. He wanted to probe it. Detective Sergeant Ringwood had given him the credit of being a keen observer, who might be useful to him in the case, and departed from his usual routine by taking him, more or less, into his confidence.

But the Sergeant would have been considerably more impressed could he have looked within the note book which Westerham took from a drawer he unlocked in his study table. In it he had noted down, and commented upon briefly, every detail and incident that he had observed or remembered in connection with the crime, from his first arrival at the garden party to the present moment. To these notes he proceeded now to add the information which Ringwood had just given him, sprawling back in his chair, smoking vigorously, and, every now and then pausing with his hand holding his fountain pen, stretched out straight in front of him, another characteristic posture of his when working out a thing in his mind.

There came a pause in his note making when the arm was held out longer than usual. He smoked more slowly. His forehead was knitted into a frown. Then he wrote these words, carefully and deliberately.

"Ringwood, after showing us the band and the fragments of the box, had another 'find'. But he changed his mind about it. He only asked what the initials 'D.G.' stood for. Major Challow suggested Diana Garforth—well—so far as I know she *was* the only one present with those initials. How had he got hold of them. By something he had found. What? Assuming it was something Diana had dropped, what would it be? She was carrying an umbrella and a vanity bag. And she wore gloves —before tea, at all events. Women don't have their initials on umbrellas or gloves, I fancy. The vanity bag would contain—" he smiled as he wrote it down, "looking glass—comb—the usual things—handkerchief. Assume she dropped her handkerchief. But any guest might have done that. There's probably nothing in it."

"When did I see her?" And the colour mounted in his cheeks a little as he wrote, "We had tea together—the Band was playing all the time. Then the people from Horton came up—a general conversation. After that I missed her—strolled down to the pools —ah, she was there—coming up from the path beyond—it was then that Nayland made that remark about Diana's pool. Was she in the hall at the concert? I didn't see her. When did she go? She was walking home, she told me."

He wrote the words again.

"Probably nothing in it!"

Then he glanced at the clock on the mantelpiece. A quarter past four.

"I'll go and see her," he said to himself, "run there in the car. If that detective chap has got any silly nonsense about her it's up to me to keep her out of it. Here goes!"

And he went.

CHAPTER 5

The Garforths were not parishioners of Westerham's. Beechcroft, their residence, was just outside the borders of Coppleswick, but only about a mile and a half from the Vicarage. Mr Garforth was a widower, a successful barrister, who went up to London most days to his work, and devoted himself to gardening and golf when at home. Diana was the only child living with him. He had two other daughters, married, and a son, but the latter rarely put in an appearance and Westerham had noticed that he was not often mentioned.

Westerham himself had only been Vicar of Coppleswick for a little over a year. He owed his promotion to the benefice, while still a young man in the twenties, to his assiduous work as curate in a large town parish where he had made a name for himself. Coppleswick was in the gift of Lord Rochdale, who owned much of the land there, and, when vacant, he had consulted the Bishop and asked him to tell him of a good man.

"Yes, I can do that," replied the Bishop, "only I don't know if the man I have in my mind would take a country living. Westerham, curate at High Ferring. He'd suit you. Capable, a gentleman, and possessed of a stock of good all round common sense—which is more than all my clergy have," he added, with a little chuckle.

Westerham had at first demurred, having never thought of a country parish, but had finally accepted, partly because he wanted more time for study, and had some idea of writing. But when he came to Coppleswick, a little apprehensive as to whether he had made a mistake, he very soon found that a large scattered country parish, with its different grades of society ranging from squire to agricultural labourer, with farmers, dealers and small tradesmen in between, offered quite as much scope for work as a town parish and called for infinitely more tact in carrying out that work. Besides, as time went on, he began to own to himself that he was very glad he *had* come to Coppleswick—for there was Diana Garforth!

Diana was four and twenty, essentially a type of the English country girl. She played a good game of golf and tennis, rode to hounds, drove a car, and was game for a ten mile walk over the hills when the mood took her. Added to this she was a first-rate housekeeper and "ran" Beechcroft admirably. Also she was, if not exactly brilliant, a well informed girl, and had had the advantage of being educated at a school modelled on the lines of a public school, with nothing "finicky" in its atmosphere. She was good company, frank and natural and without affectation.

And so it was not at all surprising that she had had half a dozen offers of marriage—but nothing had come of them.

She was standing on the steps leading to the front door when Westerham drove up in his two-seater, having apparently just come in from a walk, for she carried a stick in her hand.

"Hullo, Mr Westerham," she exclaimed, coming forward, "do you want to see father? Because he hasn't got back yet."

"No," he said, bluntly, "I want to see you."

"Very nice and charming of you. Come in and have some tea. I'm simply dying of thirst," and she led the way into the drawing room and rang the bell for tea.

"I thought perhaps you wanted to talk over this terrible affair with father," she said, "he's keenly interested. You know he specialises in criminal cases? Isn't it awful?"

He nodded.

"Have they caught—the man yet?"

"No. It's very strange, for I assure you the police are doing all they can. And they were on the spot immediately afterwards."

"Do you think they will catch him, Mr Westerham?"

"Well, I should imagine so. Policemen are pretty dogged people, you know, and they've all sorts of ways of going to work."

At this moment the maid brought in tea and the subject was dropped as preparations were being made for the meal. Then, as she poured him out a cup, Diana said,

"How is poor Miss Nayland? I nearly went to see her today, but I thought she might be too upset. I *am* so sorry for her."

"I was with her this morning. She's awfully brave about it, but it's been a horrible shock to her."

"Yes—of course."

"When did you first hear of the murder?" asked Westerham, "I suppose you had come away before it happened?"

"Oh, yes. It was late last evening when we got the news—Robert, our gardener, came to tell us."

"Yes? What time did you come away? You didn't hear the Glee Singers, did you? At least, I don't think I saw you there."

She looked at him quickly.

"No—I didn't hear them. I was walking home, you know—and I thought I'd make a start before it rained too hard. As it happened though, I got awfully wet."

He stirred his tea thoughtfully. And then came to the point.

"I'm going to ask you something," he said, "I hope you won't mind."

"What is it?"

There was just a shade of uneasiness in her voice as she asked the question. And he noticed it.

"Did you happen to lose anything at 'The Pleasaunce' yesterday?" he went on, "such as a handkerchief?"

"Why? Did you pick it up, Mr Westerham?"

He observed at once that the wording of her question implied that she *had* lost a handkerchief, and knew it.

"Because," she went on, before he could reply, "it's awfully good of you to bother to bring it back—though how did you guess it was mine?"

"Well, you see, it had your initials on it—and you were the only person with those initials there."

"How frightfully clever of you!" she exclaimed, with a forced little laugh, "you might almost be a detective! Won't you give it to me, please?"

"Whereabouts did you drop it?"

"What a silly question! Why, if I'd known where I'd dropped it I shouldn't have lost it, should I? We were wandering about all over the place. Whereabouts did you find it, Mr Westerham?"

"I didn't find it and I haven't got it," he replied. "Of course I don't imagine that there's anything in it, but I wanted you to know that it's in the hands of the detective in charge of the case."

Her eyes opened wider as she looked at him. And there was a distinct expression of fear in them.

"But surely—" she began, and then stopped.

"Please don't get worried," he said gently. "It's a very simple matter, but I wanted to—well—not exactly warn you—it's like this. Ringwood, that's the detective, you know, made a very close examination of the scene of the crime, as of course he would. And somewhere, in the wood beyond those pools of water, he found several things that are clues—and, among them, as far as I can judge, your handkerchief."

"But he *can't* think *I* have anything to do with the murder!" exclaimed the girl, sitting up in her chair and grasping its arms.

"Of course he can't," replied Westerham.

"Then what—?"

"Well, it's like this. He may have got it into his head that you may have seen something—not the actual murder, of course—that's out of the question, but Mr Nayland and this man walking or talking together. Do you see what I mean? He may want you to give evidence later on."

"But I didn't see anything, I assure you."

"That's all I wanted to know. If you had, I thought I might have helped you a bit—if you'd have let me."

"It's awfully good of you," she murmured, "yes, I see. Do you think," she went on, "this detective is likely to come and ask me questions?"

"Yes, I do," he assented, "but it needn't alarm you."

"N-no—I suppose not."

"Look here," said Westerham, kindly, "if you *did* see anything suspicious yesterday afternoon, you might tell me. I wouldn't give it away. You were in the wood?"

"Yes—I went into the wood—" she hesitated. "As a matter of fact I went home that way—it was a short cut—I came through it into the lane at the back of your Vicarage—and got into the main road by it. I must have dropped the handkerchief then. The rain was coming down hard."

"What time was that?" he asked.

"What time? Oh, I remember hearing your church clock strike six just after I got into the lane."

"You were alone, of course?"

It was a casual question, but the colour mounted into her cheeks as she replied.

"Why—yes—what makes you ask that?"

"I only meant you didn't see anyone in the wood as you came through it?"

"Of course not."

"Then that's all right, Miss Garforth. There's nothing to worry about. Just tell Ringwood, if he comes to see you, what you've told me. And I hope you'll forgive me for having bothered you about it."

"Indeed," said the girl, with a smile, "I think it's most frightfully kind of you. I know you wanted to help me."

"I should always want to do that," he answered gravely, "if you would let me."

She glanced at him quickly, hesitated, and then said.

"I know—I—ah—" she went on, "There's the car. That's Father come from the station."

The sound of a car was heard, followed by a step in the hall outside. Suddenly Diana leaned forward, and said in a low voice,

"Please don't say anything to Father about this handkerchief business."

As he nodded in assent, wondering a little, Mr Garforth came into the room, a tall, spare man, gray haired, with keen, penetrating eyes, and clear cut features, firm lips, which parted into a little smile as he caught sight of his visitor.

"Ah, Westerham," he said, "glad to see you. I understand you and Challow were the first on the scene in this horrible affair, and I want you to tell me about it. They haven't caught the beggar yet, I see!"

And he handed an evening paper to the Vicar. There it was, in broad headlines spread across the front page.

"THE COPPLESWICK TRAGEDY"
"Murderer still at large"
"Who is the mysterious 'bandsman'?"
"The Clue of the Broken Box"
"The 'Evening Gazette' offers a reward."

"Yes," went on Garforth, helping himself to bread-and-butter, "it's a stunt for the newspapers, eh? This one offers fifty pounds to any hotelkeeper or letter of lodgings who can throw any light on this foreign bandsman fellow—I suppose he *was* a foreigner? Poor Nayland! He was only dining here with his sister last Thursday. An interesting chap, Westerham, eh? Though he never talked much. Well, now, tell me all about it. I haven't heard any first hand news yet, and I confess I'm interested. It's in my line."

Whereupon a long discussion on the crime took place—so long, that Diana left the two men to themselves. Garforth, with his long experience of getting up briefs, was very soon master of all that the Vicar had to tell him.

"It sounds like a clear case," he said, offering his visitor a cigar —but Westerham preferred his pipe. "Yes," he went on, cutting his own cigar, "there's enough circumstantial evidence to hang the man. It wouldn't be an easy case to defend, and most juries would convict. Apart from the motive, which we don't know— probably poor Nayland carries the secret with him to the grave —the only really puzzling thing about it seems to be that coat business. Can you make it out?"

The Vicar shrugged his shoulders.

"Not a bit," he replied.

"Ah," went on the other, lighting his cigar, "I wonder—tell me, Westerham—you're an observant man, I fancy—was there any sign of a struggle?"

"None, that we could see."

"And this green jacket; did it look as if it had been forced on to Nayland's shoulders? You know what I mean—rumpled about, or anything like that. Or did he seem to be wearing it naturally?"

"That's not quite easy to answer," replied Westerham, "because the body was under water and we had to drag it out. But, so far as one could judge, he might have put it on himself."

"Umph! Anything in the pockets?"

"Nothing."

"When is the inquest? They haven't held it yet, I suppose?"

"No. It's tomorrow—at 'The Pleasaunce,' at twelve o'clock."

"I shall attend. It happens to be an off day. Of course they'll adjourn it. But there isn't any doubt about the ultimate verdict. Must you be going? Well, drop in again soon. Can't you run over on Sunday evening after service and have a meal? I should like to have another chat about this affair."

"Thanks very much. Yes, I'll come with pleasure."

Garforth walked to the door to see him off. Diana was not about. As Westerham got into his car, however, he saw a note with his name on it lying on the driver's seat. He said nothing, but pulled up his car by the side of the road a little later, and read it.

DEAR MR WESTERHAM:

I want to thank you again ever so much for coming this afternoon. I can see perfectly plainly how thoughtful it was of you. And this is just a line to ask you not to mention it to anyone —not that I think you *would*.

Again, thanking you awfully,

Yours sincerely,

DIANA GARFORTH.

P.S. I didn't want my father to be worried about me.

The Vicar, as he put his note in his pocket, was shrewd enough to know that the real message lay in the postscript. *Why* didn't Diana want her father to know about such a trivial thing as the dropping of a handkerchief? Why should he be worried about it?

Then, as he puzzled over it, there came suddenly into his mind the fact that Garforth was considered to be one of the cleverest cross-examiners at the Bar. Was it because Diana was afraid that her father might worm something out of her that she was trying to hold back? The very suggestion made him angry with himself. He had no right to suspect her of any subterfuge: it was the last thing he wanted to do. And yet, he could not help noticing the curious hesitation and evident alarm which she had shown that afternoon when he mentioned the affair of the handkerchief.

Pshaw! Wasn't it only natural? Of course, any girl in her place would loathe the idea of being drawn in as a witness to such a crime. And, the very fact that she *had* been close to the spot just before the murder was committed was enough to make her see things in a false perspective, to dread the mere idea of having to give any evidence.

Also, the knowing that a detective had got hold of that handkerchief, and might be building up some impossible, but unpleasant theory upon it, was, to say the least of it, unnerving. That was all there was in it.

He glanced at his watch. It was nearly six o'clock. Always, on Fridays, he had service at six in his church, so he pressed his foot on the accelerator and hurried. He had just time, leaving his car outside the church, to don cassock and surplice, and to ring the bell for three or four minutes. For, in a country parish, the parson has to do many little things which the town clergyman knows nothing of, and ringing the bell at weekday services is generally one of them.

Beneath the west end tower, where he was standing, was the chamber containing the mechanism of the clock. Before it struck it gave out a warning click. He paused in his ringing when he heard this. Then the great bell above boomed out six well measured strokes.

"Six o'clock!"

As he walked up the aisle to take the service he could not help remembering that it was just about this time yesterday that the murder had taken place. Then, just as he reached the reading desk a sudden thought followed.

There were only four or five women in the congregation, and they did not know the effort the Vicar was making to fix his mind on what he was saying and not to let his thoughts stray elsewhere. But as soon as he had finished and garaged his car he made straight for his study, lighted his pipe, took out his note book, studied it closely, a frown on his face, and then made the following tabulation.

5:30 Or a few minutes later. Glee Singers commence.
5:40 Nayland goes out of the hall.
5:45 I look at my watch, and am certain of the exact time.
6:00 From this time guests are leaving.
6:10 Or a minute or so later. Challow and I leave the house.
6:15 We find the body.

The murder must have been committed close on 6 o'clock, a few minutes before or after.

Diana Garforth says she left before the concert—to avoid the rain. But she also says it was pouring hard when she went through the wood, though it did not do that until quite ten minutes—or even more—after the concert had begun. And she says the church clock struck six when she came out of the wood into the lane.

What was she doing between half past five and six? And where was she all that time?

Westerham put the note book on the table, jumped up from his chair, and paced up and down his study—his mind greatly perturbed. He admitted to himself that he loved Diana, that he meant to ask her to be his wife, that he *could* not believe anything wrong of her. And yet, all the time, she had either blundered in what she had told him, or was holding something back. What was the meaning of it?—and—she had begged him to say nothing about that handkerchief incident. It worried him a great deal more than the problem of how Felix Nayland came to be wearing that green jacket, for that was only a problem of the head—and *this* was a problem that touched the heart.

There came a ring at the telephone that was fixed to the wall of the study. He paused in his walking to and fro and took down the receiver.

"Hullo!—yes? Yes—this is Coppleswick Vicarage—yes—I'm Westerham."

"Ringwood speaking—from police station, Sydbury."

"What is it? Have you caught him?"

"No—not yet. But a queer thing has just happened and I thought you'd like to know. I told you about Anstey?"

"The genuine violinist, yes—what about him?"

"He telephoned through to us a few minutes ago to say he'd had a letter this evening containing a five pound note—and a half sheet of paper with these words in pencil—'To provide you with a new coat.'"

"Was it signed?"

"No."

"What was the postmark? Have you asked Anstey to keep the envelope?"

A chuckle came over the telephone, and then,

"What do *you* think, sir! Give us credit for a little observation. But it's no use. It was left by hand—dropped into the letter-box. Queer, isn't it?"

"Very. It looks as if the fellow had got to London, eh?"

There came another chuckle.

"Well—we *have* thought of that, sir."

"How did he get there?"

A pause. And then, in a sadder tone of voice,

"Ah—that's where he seems to have fooled us all. Good night, Mr Westerham. You'll be at the inquest tomorrow, I suppose?"

"Yes, certainly. Good night!"

And he hung up the receiver.

"Then he *did* mean to take back that coat, apparently," he said to himself. Then a ring came at the Vicarage door. He glanced at the clock. A quarter past seven. And he had a confirmation class before supper. Half a dozen youths came crowding into the room and he settled himself to try to explain the Catechism to them. But it was not easy.

CHAPTER 6

The inquest on Felix Nayland was held in the hall at "The Pleasaunce." It was packed with people, the Coroner and his jury, representatives of the Press, both London and local, the police, a sprinkling of Nayland's friends and as many of an inquisitive public as could gain admittance, though with the limited room there were but few of the latter.

The Coroner, a Sydbury solicitor, who knew the Naylands socially, said to Miss Nayland when he came in,

"I'm afraid this is a dreadful ordeal for you. I'll try to make it as easy as possible for you, and after you've given your evidence there's no occasion for you to remain, if you'd rather not—though I'm afraid several witnesses must give their evidence before I ask you certain questions."

"It's very good of you," she replied, "but I feel I must be here. I shouldn't rest if I went out."

He nodded sympathetically, and took his seat. The jury had already viewed the body, and he addressed them briefly,

"You will bear in mind," he said, "that your only duty is to find the cause of Mr Nayland's death. If you have any questions you wish to ask witnesses they should, strictly speaking, be put through me. I should like to say at once, also, that the police have intimated that they will ask for an adjournment; and if I grant such adjournment, you will, of course, be required to meet again. It is first necessary that there should be a formal identification of the body, and I will ask Miss Nayland if she will be good enough to do this."

Very quietly she answered the few questions he put to her, and then he said,

"Thank you. If you don't mind I should like you to give us some further information presently."

She resumed her seat, and Major Challow was sworn.

"I am asking you, at this juncture, Major," said the Coroner, "kindly to give your evidence from a non-official point of view. I daresay you yourself would rather reserve the purely police evidence until a later stage?"

"That is so," replied the Chief Constable.

"Then, as I understand that you were one of those who found the body, will you kindly tell us the facts?"

Major Challow did so, in a clear, concise manner, uninterrupted by the Coroner. When he had finished the latter proceeded to question him.

"About what time was this?"

"A quarter past six. We made a note of it—Mr Westerham and I."

"When had you seen Mr Nayland last?"

"I can't exactly tell you that. There were a good many people here and one didn't take particular notice at the time."

"Quite so," said the Coroner, glancing at his notes, "another witness will give us more exact information on that point— which is important. Tell us—the body was under water?"

"All except the feet."

"As you think it would naturally have fallen after it had been stabbed?"

"That was the inference—that he pitched down the bank."

"And, as it were, slid in—head foremost?"

"Yes."

"The bank is steep?"

"Very."

"You did not at first think it *was* Mr Nayland?"

"No. I have explained to you that the green uniform coat he was wearing first attracted our attention. We naturally thought he was one of the Band which had been playing."

"And it was not until you had turned him over—when he was

out of the water—that you recognised him?"

"That is so."

"Thank you, Major, I think that's all. . . . Yes, what is it?"

"I should like you to put one more question, sir," said one of the jurymen, "would it have been possible to have identified the body as that of Mr Nayland *before* he was pulled out of the water?"

"It is rather irrelevant," said the Coroner, a little testily, for, in the course of his professional duties he had suffered much from the asking of questions that were quite beside the mark, put by jurymen who wanted to show how clever they were. "I'll put it if you wish it."

"I really can't say," replied Major Challow, a little stiffly—for he was an official himself, and wished to show that he supported a brother official in snubbing foolish non-officials. "Certainly it never occurred to us at the time. We were only anxious to get the body out of the water, thinking that the man, whoever he was, had accidentally fallen and might only be partially drowned."

"Quite so," said the Coroner, dismissing the Major with a nod. "Mr Westerham?"

Westerham had been seated next to Miss Nayland, carefully following the Major's evidence. When the juryman had put his question the Vicar's keen mind at once set to work to find an answer to it, irrelevant as it was. He might be asked the identical question himself in a few moments. So he did some rapid thinking. *Would* it have been possible to say that the body was not that of the bandsman, before it had been touched? Well, a shrewd observer, like himself, might have noticed beforehand— as he had done—that the bandsman was wearing brown shoes and trousers with a thin stripe. And the feet on the bank were in black boots, and the trousers navy blue. He ought to have thought of it himself—at the time—but—

He had taken his place now, to give his evidence. Like Major Challow, he told his story without interruption. Then the Coroner looked at his notes for a moment or two. His questions took a line different from those he had put to the Major.

"You had noticed this bandsman previously?"

"I had."

"Will you tell us, please."

Westerham told, as briefly as possible, how Nayland and he had found the man alone in the hall, just before the concert.

"Did he make any remark as to what he was doing there?"

"Yes."

"What did he say?"

Westerham told him.

"Did Mr Nayland speak to him again in the hall?"

"No."

"Do you think—er—well—that he recognised him?"

"Yes, I do."

"Why?"

"From the way he looked at him."

The Coroner glanced at his notes again.

"You are probably aware that this man was not a regular member of the Band—that he was acting as a substitute."

"So I am told."

"Is that proved, sir?" asked the juryman who had spoken before.

"It will be," snapped the Coroner, "by another witness. I mention it now for purposes of evidence. Now, Mr Westerham, was there anything which happened that would make it appear that the object of this man's visit here was to get an interview with Mr Nayland?"

"I don't think so. On the other hand, he started and looked a little confused when he turned round here and saw Mr Nayland. I would rather suggest that his object was to get away. He went out almost directly."

"And Mr Nayland?"

"He, also, went out—immediately afterwards."

"You suggest he was following the bandsman?"

"It would seem so."

"You did not actually see them together after that?"

"I can't be certain. But I fancy I caught a glimpse of the man's green jacket moving within the trees at the edge of the wood. I was standing on the terrace at the time. It was raining hard and I could not see clearly."

"Thank you, Mr Westerham."

The next witness was the doctor, a cautious man, who gave his statement carefully and slowly, proving that death was instantaneous and was caused by a stab in the back which had penetrated the heart.

"You say the whole of the blade of this knife," remarked the Coroner, taking it up from the table before him, "was buried in the body?"

"I do."

"Which would imply considerable force in driving it home to the hilt?"

"It certainly would."

Miss Nayland was now recalled. The Coroner addressed her sympathetically, and said:

"There are two or three questions I would like to ask you, Miss Nayland. I know this ordeal is very painful to you, but I am sure you will help us if you can—in the interests of justice."

"I will do my best."

"Well, then, your brother had travelled a great deal abroad, had he not?"

"Yes. He had been abroad for some years."

"Did he ever lead you to believe that he had made any enemies in his travels?"

She shook her head.

"Never," she replied.

"Or had any dangerous adventures?"

"He had had adventures, certainly. Part of the time he was on exploring expeditions. But he rarely talked about himself or what he had done abroad."

"He did not seem to be in fear of anyone?"

"Most decidedly not."

"We shall find subsequently," went on the Coroner, speaking to the jury and pointing to the fragments of the ebony box, which were lying on the table, "that it is probable that a box—of which there are the pieces—was stolen from the hall by this bandsman. I want to know, please, Miss Nayland," and he turned to her once more, "whether you can tell us anything about the box?"

"Nothing, I'm afraid. Except that it was given to my brother in June by a friend of his—a foreigner named Valdez—who came to see us and stayed a night. He said he thought my brother would like it as a memento."

"Of what?"

"He didn't say."

"Did you ask your brother?"

"Yes—afterwards."

"Did he tell you?"

"No, he only laughed, and said it was nothing much. That was his way."

"Did he appear to value it?"

"Not at all."

"You don't know where this man Valdez came from?"

"No. But since I told the police about him I remembered he wrote his name in our visitors book. I have it here."

And in the book was written,

"Ignace Valdez."

It passed round the jury, who pressed over it considerably. The Coroner dismissed Miss Nayland, with a few words of thanks, and Anstey, the nervous little violinist, took her place. He was more nervous than ever, and once or twice almost raised a laugh —which the Coroner checked sternly. The latter helped him out with his statement tactfully. Then came the episode of the five pound note, and the scrap of paper with the pencilled message on it. Both were shown round.

"You have the number of this note?" the Coroner asked the Superintendent of Police, who nodded.

"Then we may return it?"

The Superintendent nodded again. The little violinist grabbed the note hastily, evidently glad to get it back again. Then he hesitated,

"And my uniform coat," he said, "may I have that, too, please?"

"Not yet, I'm afraid," replied the Coroner grimly. And a smile lit up the faces of those who saw the little man's evident discomfiture. Pressmen made a note of it, with a view to one of those light touches in a serious case so much loved by the British public.

The butler was next called. He stood in front of the Coroner in an attitude of dignified but respectful attention, the personification of a well trained servant.

"Your name?"

"James Burt, sir."

"You are butler here?"

"Yes, sir."

"How long have you been in the service of the late Mr Nayland?"

"Since the beginning of last March. I was steward on the boat by which he returned to England, and he suggested, on the voyage, that I should take service under him, sir."

"You had not known him before?"

"No, sir."

"So that you can't tell us anything about him that may help to clear up this mystery?"

"No, sir. Mr Nayland was a very good master, sir, but, if I may say so, was not communicative to those who served him. He rarely spoke to me except in connection with my duties, sir."

"I see. Well, can you tell us what you saw last Thursday afternoon."

"Only what I have already told the police, sir."

"Quite so. That is what we want."

Gravely, and with his dominant calm demeanour, Burt made his simple statement, almost in the same words in which he had made it to Ringwood.

"Ah," said the Coroner, "so you saw your master and this man who wore the green coat, going together towards the garden, eh? You didn't follow them?"

"Of course not, sir. It wasn't my business."

71

"No. You were in the marquee all that time?"

"Yes, sir—except," he added, "that I went over to the house for a few minutes—after I had seen them."

"Thank you. That will do. Now Superintendent, I think—"

But he stopped. One of the maids had come into the hall and was speaking to the Superintendent in a low voice. Then he nodded, and said to the Coroner,

"Will you excuse me for a minute, sir? I am wanted on the telephone. They have rung me up from Sydbury."

"Very well," said the Coroner, adding, as the Superintendent went out of the hall, "we must wait a few minutes. The police are the only other witnesses."

A subdued hum of conversation broke out. The Coroner bent over the table and busied himself with the notes he had been taking. Garforth elbowed his way across the hall and came up to the Vicar.

"Very interesting case, Westerham," he said, in a low tone of voice, "there's enough evidence to hang this fellow—that's certain. But not a single word that throws any light on the mystery of the whole affair has been said by any of the witnesses."

"There's a story behind it somewhere, isn't there?" replied Westerham.

"By Jove there is! I wish—ah, here comes the Superintendent. Now we shall find out how far the police mean to go today."

There was quite a genial smile on the Superintendent's face as he re-entered the hall. He squeezed a passage towards the Coroner, and, as he passed Major Challow, who was seated at the foot of the table, leaned over him, and whispered something in his ear. The Chief Constable gave a start, and exclaimed,

"Gad! You don't say so, what!"

And then *his* face broke into a smile.

But the Superintendent had passed on, and now whispering emphatically to the Coroner. When he had finished, the latter turned to the jury.

"Gentlemen," he said, "a very important development in the

case has arisen. You will be interested to hear that the police have succeeded in tracing this pseudo bandsman—and that he is now detained by them."

A buzz of excitement ensued. Some of the reporters tried to push their way forward towards the Superintendent, who had come back to the Chief Constable and was busily engaged in consultation with him and Detective Sergeant Ringwood. One enterprising reporter, who had taken the precaution of engaging a village youth and had managed to smuggle him into the inquest, hastily pencilled a message to his editor on a telegraph form, thrust it, with some silver, into the boy's hand, and literally pushed him out of the front door with injunctions to dispatch it at once from the village post office and a promise of further reward. That was how the "Evening Gazette" published the news in quite an early edition, and scored off its rivals by nearly an hour and a half—quite an achievement in the journalistic world.

"Order, please!" cried the Coroner, sternly.

The buzz of conversation died down.

"Now, Superintendent!" went on the Coroner.

The Police Superintendent, after a final word with the Chief Constable, turned to the Coroner, and said,

"In any case, sir, we should have asked for an adjournment. But after what has happened, we feel that, at this particular juncture, we would like to reserve any evidence we were prepared to give—I'm sure you will see our point."

"Oh, I quite agree," replied the Coroner, "shall we fix upon a day and an hour for the reopening of the inquiry?"

And, in another minute he said,

"We will now adjourn. Thank you, gentlemen. You are at liberty to retire."

The reporters crowded around the little group of policemen, eagerly asking for news about the capture.

"If you'll wait a few minutes," said the Superintendent suavely, for he knew how to deal with the Press, "I shall very likely be able to give you something. I don't know much myself yet, but I'm going to get on the telephone. It's in the library, isn't it?"

"Yes," said Ringwood.

"Let's go there, what!" remarked Major Challow. "Miss Nayland, may we make use of your library, please?"

"Certainly you may, Major—and, will you please have all the people you don't want out of the house?"

"Why, of course. We ought to have seen to that." And he gave an order to a policeman on duty.

Ringwood went up to Westerham.

"I daresay you may come with us," he said, "we look upon you quite as an assistant in the case, sir—besides, we shall want you."

"What for?" asked Westerham, as they entered the library.

"Identification," replied the detective. "I expect he's only detained at present. We shall want someone to recognise him. Ah—"

For Major Challow was ringing up Sydbury Police Station. Then he put the receiver to his ear and listened—with occasional sharp questions.

"Gad!" he said, as he rang off. "Infernal cheek, what! He's detained at Scotland Yard. And how on earth d'you think he gave himself away? He's a fool!"

"Went to Marylebone Cloak Room for his bag?" hazarded Westerham, quietly.

"What?" and the Major turned on him sharply while Ringwood gave vent to a little delighted chuckle of amusement, "how the deuce did you guess that, padre? For it's exactly what he *did* do."

"Well," retorted Westerham, "you almost let it out yourself, Major. You said he'd given himself away and was a fool. And that's about as foolish a thing as a guilty man could do. It wasn't very hard to guess."

"You're too sharp, padre," said the Major, with a short laugh, "Now Superintendent, what's the next thing to do? We must have him down to Sydbury, what! Let's get him clear of these Scotland Yard people as soon as possible."

"That's all right, sir," replied the Superintendent. "We'll soon have him safe and sound under lock and key at Sydbury. Ringwood, you'd better run up to London—take Holt with you. And, of course, he'll have to be identified."

"I was thinking of asking Mr Westerham to do that, sir. He seems to have noticed him here more than anyone else."

"When do you want me?" asked the Vicar.

"Well," said Ringwood, "I hope we shall get him down to Sydbury this evening—I suppose we shall have to wait till Monday morning. Can you come in then, sir?"

"Certainly—a little after ten?"

"That will do capitally."

"You'll have to pick him out from a lot of others, you know, padre," said Major Challow, "there'll be a parade for you, what!"

Westerham walked back to his Vicarage after the inquest by the short cut through the wood. When he came to the pools he paused for a few minutes. The scene of the tragedy had a fascination for him.

It was furthest from the Vicar's thoughts to pose as an amateur detective, to emulate those creations of fiction who prove themselves, generally, far superior to the police, and are in the habit of discovering clues which the professional consistently overlooks. He knew perfectly well that Ringwood, shrewd observer as he was, must have exhausted all the clues which had been left, if, indeed they were clues—for the thought of the handkerchief came into his mind.

Again, even if Westerham had made any new discoveries he would not have acted as the amateur detective of the story books usually does—kept them to himself and triumphantly have proved the official police to have been in the wrong. He was quite aware that, in the circumstances of this particular case and of his particular position, Ringwood had probably gone a little outside the cautious policy of the police, and had, more or less, taken him into his confidence, and he was prepared to respect that confidence and to do anything he could to assist the detective.

So it was with no idea of gaining fresh information that

he stood on the path dividing the two pools and once more surveyed the scene, but rather the promptings of a natural curiosity to put "two and two" together and see exactly how they made the sum total of "four."

Ringwood claimed to have established the fact that, at some time after the rain began to fall, Felix Nayland was standing behind the tree on the further side of the upper pool. It was his footprint which had been there. Close by, the ungummed cigarette paper had been lying—not blown there, for there had been little wind that day, and, within the trees, practically none at all. And Nayland did *not* smoke cigarettes. Therefore, the inference was that the two men were standing there— Nayland and the bandsman. Yet, there was no sign of the latter's footprints; though that might have been because the soft, crepe soles had made no noticeable impression.

He tried to imagine what had taken place. Suppose the two men, seeking shelter from the rain under that tree, had been engaged in some discussion—a quarrel, presumably; that Nayland had charged the other with the theft of the ebony box —had threatened him, that they had then crossed once more to the path, to return to the house, and that the bandsman, a little behind the other, had suddenly drawn his knife and stabbed him?

But, once more, the inevitable puzzle came to the front. It was all very plausible, but it did not account for Nayland wearing the green jacket.

Unless they had changed coats while standing behind the tree. But, *why?*

He shrugged his shoulders. It was all so baffling. And, slowly walking through the wood, he made his back to the Vicarage.

CHAPTER 7

Westerham, after his evening service the next day, motored over to Beechcroft to fulfill his engagement with Garforth. Very naturally the subject of conversation at the table turned on all that had been happening at Coppleswick, especially the capture of the pseudo bandsman.

"What strikes me as odd," said Garforth, "is that you have a man who was clever enough to elude the police of a whole county, and yet has the crass stupidity to fall into what was the most obvious trap."

"You mean the claiming of his bag at Marylebone cloak room?" asked Westerham.

"Exactly. It was such a silly thing to do, wasn't it?"

"Yes—but over and over again there have been instances of very acute criminals making similar slips."

"I know. All the same, I'm rather looking forward to seeing the fellow, and hearing what he has to say. That will be at the adjourned inquest."

"Is he obliged to say anything there?" asked Diana.

"No," replied her father, "he needn't unless he likes to. Well, we shall see."

"I have to go to Sydbury tomorrow to identify him," said Westerham.

"Ah, I suppose so. We must reserve our opinion till then. He may not be the man, after all."

"Don't you think he *is* the man, Daddy?" asked Diana, her elbows on the table and her chin in her hands.

"It certainly looks like it—but we don't know yet."

"But supposing he *is*," she went on, "how will they prove that he murdered Mr Nayland?"

"Well," replied her father, "on the face of it it looks obvious, doesn't it?"

"Ye-es—but no one saw him do it."

"That isn't necessary," said Garforth, "there have been very few murders with actual witnesses of the crime itself. It is nearly always a case of circumstantial evidence. Besides," he added, argumentatively, "we don't know for certain that there was no witness."

"What do you mean?"

Garforth poured himself out a glass of wine, sipped it, and leaned back in his chair. He saw the case from his professional point of view, and talked about it accordingly.

"Why, for all we know, there may have been someone else in that wood all the time, eh?"

The girl's face turned a shade paler. She fingered the bread crumbs on the table cloth.

"What makes you think so, Daddy?" she asked. And Westerham could not help remarking the little tremor in her voice.

"I didn't say I thought so," said her father. "I was only suggesting a possibility. Why," he went on, with a little laugh, still in the argumentative mood of his calling, "their might even be another alternative. This man may be a witness himself."

"What? To his own crime?" asked Westerham.

The barrister pointed across the table at his guest, as he might have done to a witness giving evidence in a court.

"You've got to remember, Westerham, what I frequently have to instil into a jury—that English law holds a man innocent until he's proved guilty. We differ from other codes in this respect, and it's an immense advantage, not only to the man who is being tried, but in balancing the number of those who try him. Now, take the legal assumption of this fellow's innocence. It might quite reasonably—we don't know yet, but I say it *might* be a reasonable line of defence that someone else killed Nayland and that this man saw him do it—and got the wind up, so to speak—disappeared out of sheer fright."

"But who else *could* have done it?" asked the Vicar.

"Ah—we should have to prove that there *was* someone else in that wood. And, as I said just now, there *may* have been."

Diana, who had helped herself to an apple, and was slowly peeling it, said, without looking up from her plate,

"Suppose—well, that there was another man there—but that he was not known to anyone—and—that—"

"Yes, go on," said her father, smiling at her.

"And that this bandsman—were found guilty of the murder—because he couldn't prove he hadn't done it—and that *really*, he was innocent all the time?"

"I'm afraid they'd hang him," said her father grimly. "Yes, anything else?"

"Yes," went on Diana, slowly, "and suppose that there was someone else—"

Garforth interrupted her with a laugh.

"Really, Di, you're getting too complicated—and the thing is strange enough as it is. I only made the supposition that there may have been *one* other man in the wood, and now you want to drag in another. All right—what were you going to say?"

"Well," and she spoke more quickly now, as if bent upon getting her question put as soon as possible. "Suppose there *was*. And that he knew this other man was there—and didn't say anything. What then?"

"It isn't likely," replied her father, "but all I can say is that in such a case I pity the conscience of such a person, that is if he *knew* the bandsman had not done it—or even if he thought there might be a chance that he hadn't. Besides, such silence would be punishable as a crime, if it were ever found out."

"But you think all the time, that this bandsman *must* have done it, don't you?"

She put the question eagerly, looking up as she spoke. And Westerham said,

"It *does* look like it, without a doubt doesn't it Mr Garforth?"

"Oh, certainly I admit that it *does*," replied the barrister, "Everything points to it, of course. But you must expect me to see things with a legal mind, you know, and I can give no definite opinion. As I say, I want to *see* the fellow."

"I wonder why he committed the burglary first," said Diana, thoughtfully.

"Burglary? Oh, you mean running off with that little box? But it wasn't 'burglary,' Di. Burglary has, in the eyes of the law, to be committed after nine o'clock. They'd classify this by the name of larceny. Oh, by the way—"

And he launched into the story of a clever burglary, a case in which he had just been engaged.

"After all," he said, in conclusion, "people have only themselves to blame by keeping such valuables in the house. I never do. I prefer the bank to keep any things of mine I'm not anxious to lose. Come, Di—you're very silent tonight!"

The girl gave a little start.

"Wouldn't you like your coffee outside?" she said, "it's a pity to waste such a glorious evening indoors."

So they adjourned to the terrace overlooking the garden, drank their coffee, and smoked there. Diana had recovered her usual good spirits. The subject which had been engrossing their attention was dropped, and the conversation turned on golf and tennis and other lighter topics. After a bit the fading daylight warned Westerham that it was time to go. He fancied Diana returned the pressure of his hand as he said "good night." He would have liked a few words with her alone, but the opportunity had not arisen.

For he was uneasy in his mind as he drove back. He had tried to allay the suspicions which had arisen in his mind on the Friday evening, and now he found them confronting him once more. *Why* had Diana asked those questions, and why had she seemed perturbed when her father had mentioned the possibility of someone else having been in the wood? Try as he would, he could not get these thoughts out of his mind, and went to bed perturbed by them.

The next morning he motored to Sydbury to keep his appointment at the police station. Before going there, however, he wanted to cash a cheque at the bank. There were several people standing at the counter, among them Diana Garforth. One of the cashiers was in the act of handing her, across the counter, a small, sealed package. At the same time he pushed an open ledger towards her, and said,

"Will you please sign for it, Miss Garforth. We have to take a receipt."

She dipped a pen into the ink, signed in the place pointed out by the cashier, slipped the parcel into her bag, and turned, to find herself face to face with Westerham.

"You're in early," he said.

"Yes, I came in by train."

"Oh, why didn't you tell me last night? I'd have run you in with pleasure."

"Thanks awfully, I never thought about it."

"Well, let me run you back then? I've to go to the police station, you know, but I don't suppose they'll keep me long. And there isn't a train to Coppleswick till nearly twelve."

"It's frightfully kind of you, and I'd love to come. Only I'm just going up to London—catching the express."

And she glanced at her wrist watch.

"I'm sorry."

She nodded with a smile and went out. Westerham cashed his cheque and made his way to the police station.

The Superintendent received him in his office. He gave an order to the constable who had shown him in.

"We shan't keep you long, Mr Westerham," he said, "it's purely a formal matter—now, if you'll come with me I think we shall find everything ready."

There were seven or eight men drawn up in a line, supervised by a Police Sergeant.

"Now, sir," said the Superintendent to Westerham, "will you see if you can identify the man whom you saw playing in the Band at Coppleswick last Thursday."

Westerham carefully scrutinised the row of faces. But very soon made up his mind. He stepped forward and, pointing to the third man in the row, a dark haired, foreign looking fellow, who wore a small black moustache, said, quietly,

"This is the man, Superintendent. I recognise him—without any doubt."

He felt the tremendous import of these simple words. He knew that, by them, he was probably taking one of the steps which would send that man to the gallows. But he knew that he was not mistaken.

The Superintendent nodded, gravely.

"Thank you," he said briefly.

The man threw out his hands.

"But I did not kill Señor Nayland," he cried. "I have told you, once—twice—all that happened. It is one great mistake."

The Superintendent went up to him, laid a kindly hand on his shoulder, and said.

"All right, my man. You'd better not talk. You'll have plenty of opportunity later on of doing that if you want to. Yes—take him away, Mitchell."

"Yes" said the Superintendent to Westerham when they were back in the former's office, "That's the man all right—evidently. Manoel Garcia, that's what he calls himself. Oh yes—we've charged him right enough, and he's under arrest. Says he didn't do it?" and he shrugged his shoulders. "Ah, well, we expect that sort of thing, you know, sir. But it's not my business to talk about him. He'll be at the adjourned inquest, of course, and if he chooses to make a statement he can, do so there—yes, certainly, he'll be on oath—but that's nothing. The verdict, Mr Westerham. H'm! There's very little doubt about *that*. But, whatever the verdict—and we don't *always* pay much attention to a Coroner's jury—he'll have to come before the magistrates here—as I say, we've charged him already. And you can take my word for it, Mr Westerham, they'll commit him for trial, right enough."

"Do you want me any more now?"

"No, you've quite satisfied me, Mr Westerham. You'll come to the adjourned inquest, of course? We may want you again there. Mr Nayland, I hear he's to be buried today. Is that right?"

"Yes. This afternoon."

"You'll have a crowd of people there, if I'm not mistaken. Astonishing what curiosity will do, isn't it? Thank you very much. Good morning!"

The Superintendent was right. The little churchyard at Coppleswick was full of those peculiar people whom a morbid curiosity, mixed with sentiment, generally draws to the burial of a murdered man. With the exception of Miss Nayland, three or four cousins were the only mourners. Reporters were there, of course. It all added to the "story" of the crime they were writing up daily, and, as long as the sensation lasted, there was not an incident connected with it to be missed.

That evening the Vicar had a parochial committee meeting at the Vicarage, to make final arrangements for a Fete and Sale of Work which was being arranged for church funds. One or two spoke of the idea of abandoning it, after the tragedy which had taken place in the village, but the general opinion was that, after all, there could be no harm in carrying out, the following week, arrangements which had almost been completed, and which would have involved considerable expense were they to be postponed. So the committee set to work on the business for which it had been called.

Diana Garforth was a member of it. She came in late, with a murmured apology—she had only just come back from London, she said. After the meeting she lingered behind. Evidently she wished to have a word with the Vicar.

"Did you identify that man this morning?" she asked, abruptly.

"Yes," he said, "I did. There wasn't any doubt about it."

"I see. And the police are certain—he committed the murder?"

"I suppose so. They've charged him with it."

She sighed slightly—and it sounded like a sigh of relief.

"And," she went on, hesitatingly, "Did they say anything about that handkerchief?"

"Not a word."

"It was so good of you to come to me. And I'm sure you remembered what I wrote to you about my father. It would only worry him."

He looked at her for a moment. Then he said, gravely.

"Yes—I see. Look here, I don't want to be inquisitive, I think you know that. And I'm not going to ask you anything—but—about that handkerchief. I know you're worrying about it—"

"Oh, no—really—" she broke in.

Then he went on,

"I want you to believe that if there's anything I could help you in, I would. It's a bit cheering sometimes to know you've got someone who—who cares—"

She interrupted him hastily, getting up from her chair as she did so,

"Thank you ever so much, Mr Westerham. I'm sure you—I mean, it's only silly of me to bother about it. I *must* get back now. Daddy will be waiting for dinner."

"And if you want help—?"

"Yes, yes. It's frightfully kind of you. But—you can't. You see— it's all right—I only got into a bit of a fright about nothing. After all, there isn't anything in dropping a handkerchief, is there?"

"No. Only—"

"Good night, Mr Westerham. I really must run away. But— you're quite too kind, you know."

On the threshold, as he was showing her out, she suddenly paused. Then she turned to him.

"You don't think *I* had anything to do with this horrible affair?"

For a moment he laid his hand on her shoulder. Then he said:

"Of course I don't. But I *do* think that because you came through the wood just before it happened that you are alarmed lest the police should know of it and ask you to give evidence. Isn't that it?"

She gave a little nervous shiver.

"Partly," she admitted, "but—oh, it's very silly of me, isn't it?"

And, before he could answer her she was walking rapidly away.

The next morning the Vicar was busy in his study over the forthcoming Fete and Sale of Work. He had settled down to a full morning's work. Many people, because they only come across the parson on Sundays, imagine that his profession only entails one day per week of real work, but in this they are greatly mistaken. Often the work on a week day is much more exacting than the taking of services or preaching on Sundays. And the parson is rarely given credit for the many hours he spends in his study over a variety of matters which would puzzle many a business man.

A maid came in, carrying a large brown paper parcel in both hands.

"Please, sir," she said, "this has just come from 'The Pleasaunce.' And there's a note with it. Where shall I put the parcel, sir?"

"Oh, put it down here—anywhere."

She put the parcel on the floor and gave him the note, which he tore open. It was from Miss Nayland, just a few lines to say that she was sending some of her brother's clothes for the Jumble Sale in connection with the Sale of Work.

"I know you won't think me heartless," she wrote, "in parting with my poor brother's things so soon, but I feel I should like them to serve some useful purpose."

Westerham was methodical in his ways. At once he wrote a few words of thanks, to be sent to Miss Nayland. As a rule he immediately consigned to the waste paper basket all correspondence which was not worth keeping, but, as he wrote, he did not notice that a puff of wind, coming in through the open window, blew Miss Nayland's letter, which was lying on his writing table, into one of its half opened drawers.

Then he proceeded to undo the parcel. There were three or four suits of clothes and an assortment of shirts, socks, and other wearing apparel, all in very good order. Men's clothes, even if in only fair condition, always go well in Jumble sales, and he recognised that these would be a welcome addition to the stall. He rang the bell.

"Tell Peters to take this note to Miss Nayland," he said, when the maid came in. "And you can put all these things"—and he pointed to the unpacked assortment—"along with the others. They're for the Jumble Sale."

And then he settled down to his work once more. As he did so he pushed the half open drawer back into the table. And he never observed that Miss Nayland's letter was lying within it, among an assortment of other papers.

CHAPTER 8

There was as much excitement at the adjourned inquest as there was at the opening of the inquiry; perhaps more, for word had, of course, gone round that the man who was suspected of having committed the crime was likely to be present, and everyone wanted to get at least a glimpse of him. It is not every day that there is the chance of seeing a real, live murderer.

The newspapers had, of course, revelled in the "story." Reporters were there, and the usual array of press photographers. And private cameras also clicked when two policemen emerged from the saloon car which drove up to "The Pleasaunce," and a dark, nervous looking man, casting apprehensive glances from right to left, walked hurriedly up the steps between them, and was taken into the crowded hall. There had been some talk of holding the adjourned inquest in some other building, to spare, if possible, the feelings of Miss Nayland, but only the village school was available, and that would have meant closing it to the children for the day. Also, Miss Nayland herself had declared that she had no objection, and wished to do all she could to assist the official inquiry.

The Coroner, to use the newspaper phrase, "opened the proceedings with a brief speech," in which he pointed out to the jury that he foresaw no reason why they should not conclude the matter and be released that day. The evidence, he said, which he proposed to call, was that of the police—all other witnesses having already been heard, though it might be necessary for one or two of them to give additional information.

"Since we met," he added, in conclusion, the police have

effected what they consider to be an important arrest. I have no power to compel this person to give evidence or to make any statement, for he has already been charged. But, he is at liberty to do so if he pleases. Now," he went on, addressing the pseudo-bandsman, "do you wish to say anything? You are not obliged to, you know."

"Si, Señor—yes, sir," answered the man, nervously. "The officers of the police already have told me I may speak if I wish— And I wish," he added.

The Coroner looked at him, sharply.

"You understand English well?" he asked.

"Oh, yes—I do. I speak not so well as I understand it. You must excuse."

"Very well. Now, before you tell us anything I want to make it quite plain to you that what you say will be written down. You understand that?"

The man nodded.

"Yes."

"And it may be used in evidence afterwards. Do you know what I mean?"

"I think so, sir. That also the police officers told me. It is perhaps that I shall go before a judge and they will tell the judge all that I say now, is it not?"

"I see you understand. Now, you know what an oath is?"

"Ah, yes. You make me swear I shall say what is true, eh?"

"That is it."

"It is good. I wish to speak what is true."

All eyes were bent upon him as he took the oath. And then the Coroner began,

"Your name?"

"Manoel Garcia."

"What is your nationality?"

"I am a citizen of the state of San Miguel—in South America."

At these words, Detective Sergeant Ringwood, who was watching and listening intently, knitted his brows for a moment. "The state of San Miguel." Where had he heard it mentioned?

"Just a little north of Brazil," added the witness.

In a flash the detective remembered. The Scotland Yard Inspector had shown him the photograph of that man who had been mixed up in an insurrection in San Miguel. "O'Calligan." That was the name, of course!

"Where do you live?" went on the Coroner.

"I tell you. In San Miguel."

"I mean *now*—in England."

"Oh, I understand. In London. I lodge in a small hotel just near Russell Square—the 'Albion' it calls itself."

The Coroner threw an enquiring glance at the Police Superintendent. The latter nodded.

"Very well," resumed the Coroner, "you may tell us now what you wish. And then I shall ask you some questions."

Manoel Garcia bowed politely. He seemed now to have a little more self-possession.

"Thank you, Señor! I wish to say that I have not killed Señor Nayland. Oh no! It is a big mistake. Why should I kill him? Indeed I have not known he was murdered till the officers of the police have told me. And I am very sorry. I come here on Thursday. I pretend to be a musician of the Green Albanian Band. Oh yes, I do not deny it. I had a reason for which I came—a private reason. Señor Nayland found out that reason—I was not clever enough to stop him. But then he agreed with me that it was a good reason. Also he helped me to go away—through the leetle wood. It was there I saw him last, and he was quite alive. I have not killed him—no. I am innocent. That is what I wish to say."

A murmur of excitement ran round the court when he ceased, but the Coroner stopped it, sternly. Garforth, who was seated near the Coroner, facing Garcia, never took his eyes off the South American's face.

"Now I will ask you questions," said the Coroner, very gravely, "and again I warn you to be careful how you answer them."

"I speak the truth," replied Garcia, drawing himself up with dignity—for he was fast recovering his sang froid. "You write it down"—and he pointed to the clerk—"I do not fear."

The Coroner looked at his notes for a moment or two. Then he began.

"You admit you came here on Thursday under the pretence of playing the violin in the Band?"

"Yes."

"You made arrangements with one of the Band—named Anstey—to do this?"

"Oh yes. I paid him to let me take his place."

"You borrowed his uniform coat?"

"The green coat? Ah, yes."

"You arranged to give him back that coat on your return to London—at the railway station, and you put a coat of your own in this bag"—for the bag and coat were exhibited on the table —"in the cloak room?"

"That is all very true, yes!"

"How did you know that the Green Albanian Band was engaged to play here last Thursday afternoon?"

This was a crucial question. Reporters leaned forward, eagerly listening for the reply.

But, if they had expected some disclosure which threw light on the mystery, they were disappointed.

"Oh," said Garcia, "that was very simple, sir. I read it in one of your newspapers which tells of the entertainments of your nobility. It was announced that the Green Albanian Band would play at Señor Nayland's house."

The Coroner paused for a moment, in thought. And then asked,

"And you thought this would be an opportunity of getting into the house?"

"Yes," replied Garcia, shortly.

"Unknown to Mr Nayland?"

Again, "Yes."

"Why?"

"I wanted something?"

"A small black box?"

"Yes."

"Why did you want that box?"

Garcia did not answer at once. Then he said, slowly and deliberately,

"I shall not tell you, sir. You have said I am not obliged to say what I do not wish."

"Yes!" replied the Coroner, sharply, "But, now that you are on oath please remember that your refusal to reply to questions may not help you."

Garcia bowed, respectfully.

"I shall not tell you," he repeated.

"Very well. There was something in that box you wanted?"

"Yes," he said, after hesitating, "I do not mind saying that."

"What was it?"

"That is what I shall not tell you, sir," he said, using the expression again.

One or two of the jury shook their heads. Evidently they were not very much impressed so far.

"Will you tell me why you wished to get hold of this box unknown to Mr Nayland?"

"Yes, sir. I will tell you that. I wish to tell you, because it explains what already I have said. I had thought that Señor Nayland would not give the box to me if I asked him for it. That is why I came in disguise. Also I did not want Señor Nayland to know what was in the box, if I could help. Afterwards I had to explain to him. And it was all right. I need not have feared. So it was a foolish thing to come as I did," and he shrugged his shoulders and threw out his hands.

The Coroner looked at his notes again. Then he said,

"I want to get at what happened after you had taken the box. Listen, please. You came into their hall when no one was about. And you took the box. And then Mr Nayland came in and spoke to you. Is this true?"

"Yes. Just as you say it."

"Very well. And Mr Nayland recognised you?"

"Yes, sir. At first I did not think so. Soon, however, I knew."

"He had known you before?"

"Yes."

"Where? In South America?"

"Yes."

"In San Miguel?"

"Yes."

"I must be plain. Did he suspect you of being a thief?"

Garcia drew himself up with dignity.

"I am of what you call good family, sir," he retorted, "I am not a thief, no!"

"Yet you stole this box?"

"That is different!"

"Very well. We will go on. After you had taken the box, and Mr Nayland had recognised you, you went out on the lawn?"

"Yes."

"And were going towards the garden?"

"Yes."

"Why?"

Garcia spoke very slowly as he replied,

"There were two reasons," he said, "first I wanted to be alone, and then—well, I was afraid of some one."

"Of whom? Mr Nayland?"

Garcia shook his head.

"No—of someone I had just seen—on the terrace outside. I wanted to get away from him."

"Why?"

"I can not tell you, sir."

"Well, who was he?"

"I will not say."

"You are foolish," remarked the Coroner, drily, "do you recognise that there is a possibility of you're being tried—of going before a judge."

"Perhaps, sir. If it is so I may have to tell. But now—no!" And he threw out his hands.

"I will not press you. Now—did Mr Nayland follow you?"

"Yes."

"And spoke to you?"

"Yes."

"And you stood together under a tree, close to one of the pools in the garden?" asked the Coroner, very sharply, after a glance at his notes.

"Oh no, Señor!" replied Garcia, "we did not stay beside the pool. I will tell you—"

"Wait, please!"

The Coroner paused. Once more he looked at his notes. Also the Superintendent, who had been whispering with Ringwood, had scribbled something on a bit of paper and passed it to the Coroner. The latter read it. And nodded.

"I am going to ask you to tell us what happened after Mr Nayland had spoken to you. But there is a question I want to put to you first.

"Do you know a man named Ignace Valdez?"

Garcia hesitated, and then said.

"He gave the box to Señor Nayland."

"Quite so. But answer my question, please. Do you know him?"

"Oh—yes—but not very well."

"Can you tell us where he is?"

"No, sir. I think he is in Spain."

"Very well. Now go on. Tell us what happened."

"Señor Nayland spoke to me, and asked me why I had come and what I was doing. As he had discovered me I told him—it was for the box. He did not know what I wanted the box for— and Señor Valdez, who gave it to him had not known. There— there was something of importance, in a secret place in the box. I explain to Señor Nayland, and he understand—oh—no—he was not at all angry with me, only he said I should have told him before—and I said I could see that. I also explain I was in fear— I do not want to go back and be near the house. He went with me by the water and into the wood beyond—and he say there is a way out at the back—he helped me, you see, to go away. First, to show him I did not lie I break open the box with a big stone— I did not know how to find the secret opening. And he saw I was

93

right. Then he say I could not run away in a green coat—and he took off his own coat—and I put it on."

There was a sensation at this. Garforth happened to catch Westerham's eye, and both men arched their eyebrows—as if questioning each other.

"Go on," said the Coroner, curtly.

"It was raining, and Señor Nayland did not wish to get wet. He say he put on the green coat to protect himself. Yes, sir—he laughed, and say they would think he had joined the Band. Then he say, while I run away he will go back to the house and give the coat to the Conductor—and—he say too—he will find this—this —this man whom I fear and prevent him from following me."

"Why would he want to follow you?" interrupted the Coroner, sharply.

"He may have suspected why I had come—it was, of course, the only reason why he could be there—and if he knew what I had found—he would have taken it from me. Perhaps he would have killed me."

Again Westerham and Garforth exchanged glances—as if the same thought had suddenly entered their minds.

"He say this—this man have no business here. There was a big official of the police present, who knew himself to be important"—The Chief Constable coloured slightly, and more than one person present grinned delightedly at the description, "perhaps he would tell the police official of this man. So he left me. And that was the last I saw of him—as he went back through the wood—in the coat I had worn. Never, *never* did I kill him, sir. It is the truth!"

"What happened afterwards? What did you do?"

"I came out of the wood into a little road, and I ran along it. You see, I had still much fear. Señor Nayland may not have stopped this—this man from following me. So I run very fast—into a big road that mounted a hill. And up the hill there was travelling very slowly, a gr-r-rand—a large motor car, with sacks it was carrying. The driver could not see me—and I climbed in behind and hid myself among the sacks. And so," he threw out an arm, "I got back to London."

"Gad!" whispered Major Challow to the Superintendent, "that's how he got away, eh? I believe he's speaking the truth *there*, what!"

The Superintendent nodded.

"Must have done it before you discovered the body, sir. A quick start."

There was a slight pause. The reporters were scribbling for all they were worth. Garcia may have been a fine liar—that was not their business—but his "story" was copy of the first water, anyhow.

The Coroner looked at Garcia keenly.

"Is that all?" he asked.

Garcia shrugged his shoulders.

"Yes, sir."

"And you say that you had not heard that Mr Nayland was murdered till the police told you?"

Garcia bowed.

"Yes," he said.

"Not when it was in all the newspapers?"

"I did not read the newspaper. I had other things to do."

"And you thought that Mr Nayland was going to give your green coat to the Conductor of the Band—to take back to its owner?"

"I thought so, yes. He had said he would."

"Then why was it," asked the Coroner, amid a tense silence, "that you sent Anstey—the owner of the coat—five pounds to buy himself a new one?"

"I did *not!*" replied Garcia.

"You didn't leave or send an envelope with a letter in it—and the money?"

"Oh, no! It is not true!"

The Coroner's lips twitched, almost imperceptibly.

"That will do," he said abruptly. "Major Challow, you would like me to take the evidence of the police?"

The Chief Constable nodded.

"If you please, Mr Coroner," he replied.

Detective Sergeant Ringwood took the oath, and gave his evidence—as much of it as the police were prepared to put forward, in a business-like manner. It amounted to little more than the police knew already—the finding of the false beard and the ebony box, Garcia's arrest, and so forth. Of the cigarette paper and the footprints he said nothing. The Coroner asked him but few questions. He knew very well that, whatever the verdict that day, Garcia would be brought before the magistrate and probably committed for trial, and that it was the policy of the police to reserve certain information, of which he was privately aware, until the prosecution. He knew, also, that the only business which concerned him and his jury was the finding of the actual cause of death.

He pointed out this in his brief and concise summing up, after asking if the police wanted a further adjournment, to which Major Challow replied in the negative.

"You have heard the evidence," he said, "and you will probably agree that it has thrown considerable light upon this inquiry. Please remember that you are not asked to find motives for the crime—that investigation belongs to its own particular legal department. Your duty is simply to say what you consider was the cause of Felix Nayland's death. I will ask you to find your verdict, and a room has been set apart to which you may retire for that purpose."

They were not very long in coming to an agreement. In less than fifteen minutes they returned. And when the Coroner asked for their verdict the foreman replied:

"We are all agreed, sir, that Mr Nayland met his death by being stabbed by Manoel Garcia."

"You mean, 'Wilful murder, against Manoel Garcia?'"

"That is so, sir."

"Very well. It shall be duly recorded. The inquiry is closed."

"But I am innocent, sir—it is the truth!" cried Garcia.

The Coroner merely signed to the police. One of them laid a hand on Garcia's shoulder—in five minutes time the police car was running him back to Sydbury.

People came streaming out of the inquest, discussing it excitedly. London reporters made a rush for station or post office, Garforth and the Vicar came out together, strolled on to the lawn, and began filling and lighting their pipes.

"What do you think of it?" asked Westerham.

"Queer, precious queer," replied the barrister, thoughtfully.

"And the verdict?"

"Oh, *that!*" exclaimed Garforth, a little contemptuously, "no jury, under the circumstances could have found any other verdict. But this is only the beginning of the real case. I'm more interested than ever in it. Whether this Garcia was lying or not, there's a funny story behind it all—and I wonder if it will ever come out."

"You think Garcia was lying?"

"I haven't formed any opinion yet. It's like reading a brief— I want to think it over quietly. When I've done so I'll be glad to have a chat with you, Westerham. I may drop in for a smoke tonight."

"All right. I shall be in all the evening." Westerham turned to go, passing the front door as he did so. The butler was standing on the step, just outside. The Vicar spoke to him.

"Well?" he said, "you've heard the verdict I suppose, James?"

"Yes, sir. And I'm very glad. I hope they'll hang him, sir."

"Ah, well—he's got to be tried first. What did you think of his evidence?"

"I didn't hear it, sir," replied the butler. "I understood I should not be wanted, and I had my duties to perform. May I ask, sir, what will be the next procedure?"

"Oh, I suppose he'll be brought before the magistrates at Sydbury to begin with—and probably they'll remand the case for the police to make further inquiries—to find out something about him, if they can. Then, if he's committed for trial, he'll be brought up at the Autumn Assizes."

"Shall I be required to give evidence, sir?"

"I should think probably you will—just the little you saw. Good afternoon."

"Good afternoon, sir, and thank you," replied the butler, with a ceremonious little bow.

CHAPTER 9

Garforth went round to see the Vicar that evening, as he had said, and the two men discussed what had taken place that day in detail.

"I confess," said Garforth, as he smoked thoughtfully, "that I am extremely puzzled—and immensely interested. As you know, my practice has been built up chiefly on criminal lines, and I suppose I may say, without boasting, that I am somewhat of an expert."

Westerham nodded.

"You've made a big name for yourself," he said, "we all know that."

"Well—I know something about the subject of crime and criminals, anyway," replied the older man, "and I can honestly say that I've tried to be fair. I want to be convinced in my own mind of the guilt of any man whom I prosecute, and of the innocence of any man I defend."

"I'm quite sure you would."

"Now, of course," went on the other, "in this particular case I'm only an interested outsider. But it attracts me very much. Not only, as I told you before, because Nayland was a neighbour of mine, but because of the unique aspect of it. For, don't you see, that whether this man Garcia is guilty or innocent, that makes no difference to the mystery of it. We're still in the dark about that."

"Do you think him guilty?" asked Westerham.

"I told you I wanted to consider the thing. Well, I have. And I want to talk it out with you. You're an observant man, and I want you to tell me what *you* think."

"It's very kind of you to have such a good opinion of me."

"My dear fellow—that's all right. Now, try to follow me. Take the facts against Garcia, for they are very strong. He was seen to go towards the garden with Nayland—we have the butler's evidence for that—and Nayland was never seen alive again. Garcia makes his escape immediately, and his description of the manner of it was probably true, and Anstey receives a five pound note to cover the cost of his coat. What does that look like?"

"Why," said Westerham, "that Garcia knew the coat would not be returned by the Conductor of the Band, that it was probably ruined by being under water and cut, and that Anstey might hold his tongue if he received compensation."

"Exactly. And it points to the assumption that Garcia had murdered Nayland, doesn't it?"

"Yes—of course it does."

"Well, assuming this, there's Garcia's story. And that would be a pack of lies—as the jury evidently thought it was."

"Yes—I know. You mean it was a preposterous story for an innocent man to tell?"

"They evidently took it in that way. And, according to their lights they were right. You've no idea what absolutely silly stories a guilty man will tell. Over and over again that alteration in the criminal law which allows the accused to give evidence recoils on him with deadly effect, just because he makes an absolute fool of himself. And if he *doesn't* choose to give evidence, he arouses the suspicion of the jury at once. This man would have done so today if he hadn't spoken. I tell you, there was never a more deadly law framed against a guilty man than allowing him this choice. It isn't always easy for an innocent prisoner—as I know very well."

"Now, then," he went on, "let us take the other point of view—the facts in his favour. Begin with his own story. I've tabulated it into plausible statements, and—for want of a better name—far fetched statements; those which impose on the credulity of one's commonsense. Here you are, look it over for yourself."

Westerham took the paper which Garforth handed to him, and read the following brief analysis.

A. PLAUSIBLE STATEMENTS

1. The changing of the coats (so far the *only* natural hypothesis which accounts for their being changed).
2. The breaking of the box in Nayland's presence. For this corroborates what he said about Nayland not knowing the contents of the box.

B. FAR FETCHED STATEMENTS

1. That there was someone present whom he feared. And there were only guests present.
2. That he would not or could not say who this individual was.
3. That he would not say what was in the box.

All these are 'far fetched' because they make it appear that he could not satisfactorily fill in the gaps in a hastily invented story.

"Yes, I see," said Westerham, when he had finished reading, "And —what else?"

"Well, the one great point in his favour was the taking that bag out of the cloak room. It corroborates his story that he did not know of the murder—or that the police were after him. Let us go further, on the assumption of St Augustine, 'credo, quia incredibile est,' and assume that the apparently unbelievable is true—that there *was* someone of whom he was afraid, and that he has very good reasons for keeping his mouth shut about it— he hinted, you remember, that he was even in danger of death. What then? Can you see the inference?"

Westerham smoked thoughtfully for a moment or two, and then said,

"Yes—I can. It's occurred to me before. The inference seems to be that if Garcia did not murder Nayland, someone else did— thinking he was Garcia, because he was wearing the green jacket. Is that it?"

Garforth nodded, gravely.

"That is it!" he agreed.

"And the murderer was this mysterious individual of whom Garcia spoke?"

"Exactly."

"Yes—" assented Westerham, slowly, "it's a possible hypothesis."

"Do you know," replied Garforth, taking his pipe from his lips, "I'm inclined to use a more definite adjective. It's a very *plausible* hypothesis—it covers pretty nearly everything, except—"

"Except what?"

"That pencilled message to Anstey—with the five pound note. But, putting that on one side, I feel sufficiently impressed with this hypothesis to under-value the defence—if it should be offered me. Of course I should want to know first the name of this mysterious individual, what was in the box, and the reasons for concealing it. Very likely when Garcia recognises that he is on trial for his life he'll disclose all this. I fancy, somehow, Nayland could have told us—poor chap. The clue to it all probably lies in South America—in this little state of San Miguel. These states are hotbeds of intrigue—mostly political—and crime. I want to know who Ignace Valdez is, too."

"Would you really take up the case, Mr Garforth?"

The older man laughed.

"Oh, well," he said, "I don't suppose it's likely to be offered to me. But I really mean what I say. I am profoundly impressed with Garcia's story—not in the way in which the police look at it. Ah, by the bye, Westerham, you're in touch with this Detective Sergeant. Couldn't you have another chat with him about it?"

"I might—certainly."

"Well, if you do, tell him plainly he may not have so good a case as he thinks he has. I wonder how this mysterious individual got to the garden party. I wasn't there, you know. Here's where your faculty of observation comes in. Do you remember all the people who were there?"

"Not I. There was a whole crowd, and lots of folk I'd never seen before. Even Major Challow, who prides himself on knowing everybody worth knowing in the county confessed there were some who were strangers to him. He pointed one of them out to me, by the way."

"What was he like?"

"There you have me, Mr Garforth—I remember he was wearing a brown suit, but, for once, I didn't particularly notice him."

"H'm, well, we might perhaps get a list of the guests who were asked from Miss Nayland, and go through them. I must be off now. See you again soon."

The next day Westerham called at the police station, but was told that Ringwood was at his home—off duty. Asking for his address, he went to a small house in the suburbs of Sydbury, where he found the Detective Sergeant busy in the little garden in front. He asked the Vicar in, offering him a cup of tea, which the latter accepted.

"Well, sir," he said, "have you come to bring me any fresh news? Though I don't think we need very much more now," and he smiled complacently, the smile of a man who has accomplished his object and is satisfied.

"Not exactly," replied Westerham, "so you think you've got your man, do you?"

"Well, don't you, Mr Westerham?" and his eyes opened a little in surprise.

"How about his own version—at the inquest?" asked Westerham, evasively.

The detective laughed.

"A very thin story, sir! It didn't go down with the jury, did it?"

"But it *did* account for Nayland wearing that green jacket."

Ringwood shrugged his shoulders.

"Very clever!" he said, "But I don't think it'll do," and he shook his head.

"Did he tell you that story before he told it at the inquest?" asked Westerham.

A cautious expression spread over the detective's face. It is one thing for the police to call in civilian aid and to take outsiders into their confidence, before they have caught a wanted man, but quite another thing as soon as they hold their prisoner and are engaged upon the evidence against him.

"That I am not at liberty to tell you, sir," he replied, "it is in the hands of my superiors."

"I see," answered Westerham, beginning to understand that it would not be so easy to get information at this stage, "how about that knife? I meant to ask you before if you had found any finger prints on it."

Ringwood shook his head.

"I'm afraid you mustn't ask me that, Mr Westerham. I've been very glad of your help, and of some of your suggestions, but on certain matters, at this stage, we are bound to hold our tongue. Now, if there's any more information you have to give me, I'll be only too glad—"

"There is," interrupted Westerham. "I see your point, and I won't be inquisitive. You're doubtless pretty certain that you've got a clear case against Garcia—"

The detective nodded

"But there *may* be an alternative, you know. The man's story may have something in it all the time."

"That's for the judge and jury to decide, sir."

"Quite so. But it's as well to be prepared. I've been talking the matter over with a person whose profession lies in the study of criminology, and he thinks there are many points in Garcia's favour. So do I, now I've considered them."

"And what are they, if I may ask?" said Ringwood, interested, but still sceptical.

"I'll tell you."

And he proceeded, step by step, to put the case in Garcia's favour, as it had been analysed by Garforth. The detective listened attentively.

"So that," he said, when Westerham had finished, "on this hypothesis somebody else killed Nayland, thinking all the time he was killing Garcia?"

"Yes."

"Um! rather unlikely!"

"Why?"

"Oh, well! But who else could it have been?"

"You don't know all the people who were there."

"True. But they were guests of Mr Nayland and his sister."

"Not necessarily."

"How?"

"It was a large garden party. Anyone might have come in and mixed in the crowd."

"Ye-es. As a matter of fact Miss Nayland gave me a list of all those who had accepted."

"She did? Well, mightn't it be worth while finding out exactly who was there. *I* couldn't tell you! Even Major Challow saw one person, at least, a fellow in a brown suit, whom he didn't know."

The detective thought for a minute. And then said,

"I don't know that it's worth the trouble, sir. But if you're really keen upon it—and it's any amusement to you," he went on, a touch of sarcasm in his voice, "I'll have a copy of that list typed and sent to you."

"Thank you," replied Westerham, "I should like it very much," and got up to go. The detective hesitated,

"Only," he said, "you'll be fair to me, won't you, sir? If you *do* find out anything you'll let me know?"

"Certainly I will. My only object is to give you any help I can."

"I know that, Mr Westerham—thank you very much for coming."

When the Vicar had gone, Ringwood went back to his room, relit his pipe, and thought hard, consulting his note book from time to time. The truth of the matter was that he had been a little uncertain—or rather unsatisfied—in his own mind before Westerham came, though he was not going to show it. He believed, quite honestly, that Garcia was guilty, but, with his long experience of crime and law he knew the importance, from the police point of view, of every jot of evidence for or against a prisoner. He wanted to be *certain*.

At length, looking at his watch, he gave, through the window, a regretful glance at his unfinished task in the garden, got up, put on his hat, and proceeded to the police station, where he was shown in to the Superintendent's office. The latter had his ear to the telephone, and only nodded. Then he put down the receiver, and said,

"The Major has just 'phoned from his house to say he's coming round in a few minutes—something fresh in the Coppleswick affair, he says. You've come at the right moment, Ringwood, to hear what he has to say."

"Then I'll wait till he comes to say what *I* have to say, sir."

In five minutes time Major Challow was with them.

"Ah, Ringwood," he said, "any news?"

"I've just had a visit from Mr Westerham, sir, and he's set me thinking a bit."

"Ah! sharp fellow, that padre!" exclaimed the Major, "What's he been up to? Hunting about for clues?"

The detective briefly told them of the suggestions thrown out by Westerham.

"You see," he added, "what worries me a bit is those finger prints."

"You didn't tell him anything about that?" asked the Superintendent, sharply.

"Not I, sir."

"Ah," said the Superintendent, "I know. Of course the fact that the knife was in the water was unfortunate. It was such a broken impression they managed to get at the Yard, wasn't it?"

"And when you compare it with Garcia's finger prints, it doesn't help much," said the detective.

"Oh, well," remarked Major Challow, "if the evidence isn't strong enough, of course we can't put it in. But, looking at it from the other point of view, it doesn't prove that the print of the knife was *not* Garcia's, does it?"

"I—don't—know," said Ringwood, slowly, "as the Superintendent says, the print on the knife is broken and poor, but you look at the photographs, sir. It seems to me that they don't exactly tally. I don't profess to be an expert, though."

The Superintendent unlocked a drawer and produced the

photographs, together with the usual magnifying glass used by the police for studying finger prints. The first photograph was that of the print found on the knife.

Finger prints are due, of course, to the markings on the fingers, no two of which are alike in individuals. A very dry surface, naturally, does not always receive a very good impression, but what marking there is is due to the slight greasiness of the skin. In this particular instance the knife handle had been under water, but Ringwood, when he carefully put it away, hoped that if the moisture were allowed to dry naturally it might still leave the greasy impression untouched, just as when one slightly greases one's finger and puts it under water, the water, if cold, does not remove the grease. In his hopes, however, he was only partly rewarded. An expert at Scotland Yard had manipulated the delicate experiment, but the result was only what the Major was looking at through the glass, faint and broken, mere patches of the imprint of a human thumb.

The other photograph showed, on the other hand, the imprint of Manoel Garcia's thumb, taken for comparison—plain and perfect. Major Challow turned the glass on to this, and presently said,

"I'm not an expert either, Ringwood. But I'm going up to London one day this week, and I'll take these with me to the department at Scotland Yard, and see what they have to say. So this lynx-eyed parson suggests that some other man, meaning to kill Garcia, knifed Nayland by mistake, What! Very plausible! Did he go on to tell you who it was? I shouldn't be surprised," he added, with a laugh.

"No sir. But he did mention that he might have wormed his way in among the guests—he even said there was a fellow there whom you did not recognise."

"Eh, what! Oh, yes—I remember asking Westerham if he knew him. But that's preposterous."

"You'd know him again, sir?"

"I think so. Possibly. Very likely a friend of one of the families asked. Well now, look here—both of you. I've just had news that I confess lets us down a bit. It came by this afternoon's post—delivered at my private address. Here it is: read it, Superintendent."

And the latter read as follows:—

105 Ellerslie Road,
Surbiton.
August 19, 1926.

DEAR SIR,

I have just read the account of the inquest held at Coppleswick yesterday on the body of Felix Nayland, murdered there, and I am interested in the evidence given by the man, Manoel Garcia, who was found guilty, by the Coroner's Court, of the crime in question. My judgment, of course, is only that of an outsider, but while it seems to me that he told an almost unbelievable story, it is only fair to him to say that in one particular he was correct, and I am in a position to substantiate this.

He denied that he left an envelope containing a five pound note and something scribbled on paper, at the house of Anstey, the bandsman whom he personated. This is perfectly true.

I have known Anstey for many years. He is an unfortunate fellow, who has seen better days, and come down in the world, but has still his feelings of pride. I called on him the other afternoon, and found him very much upset concerning his green, uniform coat, which figured in the tragedy. Probably he was exaggerating, but at any rate he said the coat was hopelessly ruined, that meanwhile he was without uniform, had been reprimanded by his Bandmaster for his foolishness, and could not afford to buy another. He was afraid, he said, of being dismissed from the Band in consequence. I pointed out to him that he had received £10 from his substitute, but he said he had paid that away—he owed it.

I wanted to do the poor fellow a good turn, I knew his peculiar pride, so determined to act anonymously. After I left his house,

I slipped the note and a pencilled message in an envelope, and thrust it through his letter box. I enclose my card, and am of course, willing to give evidence in due course if called upon.

Believe me,

Yours faithfully,

HARTLY PERRIVALE.

To MAJOR CHALLOW,

Chief Constable of Downshire,

Sydbury.

"What dy'e think of that, eh Superintendent?" asked the Major.

But the Superintendent and Ringwood shook their heads in silence. They were beginning to get puzzled again.

CHAPTER 10

If the crowd of Sydbury people who squeezed themselves into the little court presided over by the local magistrates expected that they were going to enjoy several hours of sensation they were mightily disappointed when Manoel Garcia appeared there. It was a matter of reading the indictment, the brief response of "Not Guilty" on the part of the prisoner, and formal evidence by the police of his arrest. No witnesses had been cited. Immediately afterwards the police asked for an adjournment, which was at once granted, and Manoel Garcia hurried away from the curious eyes which were gazing on him.

Major Challow, as soon as the court rose, took his intended journey to London, and took with him the photographs of the finger prints. But the cautiously delivered opinion of the Scotland Yard expert did not help him very much.

"As you say," he remarked, "the original impression is very faint and ragged. I noticed that when I took it. And I am bound to say that such portions as *do* appear do not coincide with the prints of Garcia's fingers afterwards taken. There is not enough evidence here."

"You think they don't coincide? What!"

The expert examined them once more, through powerful glasses. Carefully he measured them with delicate calipers.

"Yes—" he pronounced, "I think I may undertake to say definitely that they are not the same."

Major Challow uttered a little exclamation savouring both of annoyance and disappointment. He knew well the value of this evidence which he had lost. He also knew the very serious doubt it raised; not that it was proof positive that Garcia had never handled the knife—someone else's impression might have remained while his was lost—but it was a very grave flaw, all the same, in the case for which he and those under him were responsible.

Next he asked to see the Inspector who had been interviewed by his detective, in the hope of gaining some information with regard to any South American suspects. He had brought with him a photograph of Manoel Garcia, taken at Sydbury, but the Inspector did not recognise it.

"You'd better have a look through our list, all the same," he said, producing the files he had shown to Ringwood, "by the way, though, Garcia's room at the hotel was searched, I suppose?"

"Oh, certainly."

"Nothing found there?"

"Nothing of the slightest importance. Only clothes and a few personal belongings."

"No letters or papers?"

"Not one."

"H'm well, here you are, sir," and he handed the files to the Major. The latter turned them over in silence. Suddenly, however, he started, and exclaimed,

"Gad! Inspector, who's this fellow?"

"Let me look, sir—oh, that's O'Calligan, a half breed. Pretty bad record. I was telling your man about him the other day."

"But," said the Major, excitedly, "he was at Nayland's garden party that day. I saw him. I remember asking the Vicar who he was. Wearing a brown suit of clothes and bowler hat."

The Inspector whistled.

"By Jove!" he cried, "that's strange. How did he get there?"

"I don't know. I put him down at the time as a fellow who was staying, with some guest—who brought him there."

"Look here, sir," said the Inspector, "Nayland had South American friends, didn't he? Well, he might have asked him—we don't know. Can you get a list of the invitations sent out?"

"We've got one, already. Miss Nayland gave it to us. We didn't attach much importance to it at the time."

"Quite so, but it might help you now."

"Yes, yes," replied the Major, "but surely Nayland would never have asked a bad lot—as you say this O'Calligan is—to his party?"

The Inspector smiled.

"He might not have known he was a bad lot," he replied, "as a matter of fact, few people do. He was Secretary to Gonzolez, who led an insurrection in San Miguel and was, for a time, President. O'Calligan, to use a common phrase, 'mixed with the best society,'—if they've got any 'best society' out there. You can quite imagine Nayland meeting him at social functions, and so forth, and not in the least knowing he was really a political scoundrel. When he was over here, for instance, he stayed at a West End hotel, and was taken up by quite good people."

"When he *was* here?" asked Major Challow, "isn't he in England now, then?"

"No, he left a few days ago. He's in Paris at the present moment —or *was* there yesterday."

"Have you anything against him?"

"No. We just know his political record, which is as bad as it can be. Blackmail was one of his little dodges out there. No, he's one of those fellows we prefer to keep under a certain amount of observation when they appear in this country. But we've nothing against him."

"They don't want him *there?*"

The Inspector laughed.

"Not on an extradition warrant. It isn't a case for their police. But there *are* folks in San Miguel, I should guess, who'd be glad to see him back—for the pleasure of sticking a knife into him. It's a merry little way they have!"

The Major drummed upon the table with his fingers.

"It seems to be a merry little way they have here, too," he retorted grimly, "but all this raises a serious question, Inspector."

"H'm, yes. I see what you mean, sir. I read Garcia's story that he gave at the inquest—and if O'Calligan was on the spot, why

112

Garcia may have been speaking the truth when he said there was some fellow there he was afraid of. A fresh hypothesis, eh?"

"Yes," assented Major Challow, "it looks like it, I admit. At all events it complicates matters, and I must see into it, what!"

The following day was the occasion of the Coppleswick Church Fete, and Major Challow had promised Westerham that, if he were able to do so, he would put in an appearance. The Major was a keen supporter of the church in the district, his wife was going to open the fete in the early afternoon, taking train to Coppleswick, and he announced to her his intention of running over in his car in the early evening and bringing her home.

He took the opportunity, however, of calling at "The Pleasaunce" first. He wanted information from Miss Nayland, and, partly from motives of delicacy, he preferred seeing her as a friend, to sending one of his men. So, very soon after he was with her, he said,

"I want you to tell me something, Miss Nayland. Did your brother ever happen to mention a man named O'Calligan—whom he may have met in South America?"

"Not that I remember," she replied. "At all events I never heard him mention such a name."

"He wasn't asked here among the other guests—at your garden party? I know his name isn't on the list you gave to Sergeant Ringwood, but I thought perhaps you—or your brother might have asked him, all the same?"

"Oh, no. I'm quite sure he wasn't asked."

"Were there any people here that day whom you didn't know?"

"Yes—I think there were. Mrs Leigh-Hulcott brought a cousin who was staying with her—and the Kensworths had some friends. There may have been others, but, in the crowd, it was really difficult, at times, to be polite to each guest—and I really can't remember."

"I see; yes, I see. Well, I'm going on to this fete now—in the Vicarage grounds. I've got to find my wife there, and take her home, what! I dare say they'll rook me a bit before they let me escape."

"I should like to have been there," said Miss Nayland, shaking hands with him, "but—of course—you understand. However, I'm sending all my domestics, they've gone already, except one maid, and as soon as she's given me tea I shall let her go. Goodbye, Major."

The fete was in full swing when Major Challow reached the Vicarage grounds, and paid his six pence for admission. On one side of the lawn, shaded by trees, was a row of stalls, presided over by busy parishioners, various articles of "work," useful, or inane, sweets, toys, and the "Jumble Stall" with every conceivable article upon it from wearing apparel down to cast off kettles and broken china ornaments.

Tea tables stood in a corner of the large garden, a Band played in another, not the "Green Albanian Band," or anything like it, but the "Coppleswick Star Band," the big drum and a trombone predominating.

In a small meadow, reached by a gate connecting with the lawn, were the various "side shows," all designed with the view of catching the nimble penny or two pence, with the offer of prizes which were not so easily to be won as they appeared to be. A cocoanut shy, of course, bowling for a pig—the said pig being displayed in a small enclosure to tempt would be winners —"hoop-la," which consisted of throwing wooden rings over articles spread on a board, any articles cleanly "ringed" to be claimed by the thrower, a "dart" competition—a board divided into numbered spaces, to be thrown at by sharp pointed darts, three for two pence, anyone scoring over twenty with his three throws to receive a packet of cigarettes as a reward; a "treasure hunt," a "wheel of fortune," and, as in natural conjunction with the latter, a small tent close by where one could get to know one's character by the payment of one shilling to a palmist in gipsy attire—the said palmist, if one could recognise her beneath a browned skin and a gaudy kerchief head dress sparkling with sequins, being Diana Garforth.

The Vicar, wearing a grey flannel suit and straw hat, energetic and alert, was duly playing his part—here, there, and everywhere, seeing that all was going smoothly. It was some little time before Major Challow, escaping from the wiles of sundry stall holders, managed to get hold of him.

"I want a word with you, padre, if you can spare me a few minutes."

"All right,—come into the house—I shall be glad of a quiet smoke. And I can give you a whisky and soda, if you'd like one."

"I should," replied the Major, "it's deuced hot, what!"

"Now then," he said, when he was seated in the Vicar's study and had refreshed himself with a long drink, "what I'm going to say is in strict confidence. You can hold your tongue, padre?"

"Part of my business," replied Westerham.

"Well, do you remember, at poor Nayland's garden party, my drawing your attention to a fellow in a brown suit, and asking you if you knew him?"

"Perfectly." And he wondered what was coming.

"You didn't happen to notice his movements afterwards?"

"Sorry—but I didn't."

"Didn't see him go into that queer garden with the wood beyond, any time just before the murder—while the Glee Singers were at it?"

"No."

"Pity," remarked the Major—"or afterwards?" he asked, suddenly, as if struck by some thought.

The Vicar shook his head.

"You see," went on Major Challow, half soliloquising, "if either of us had seen him afterwards, we should pretty well have known if he'd been away from the rest, that is, if we'd noticed it."

"How?" asked Westerham.

The Major gave vent to a short laugh.

"Not so observant as usual, padre!" he chuckled, "why, his brown suit would have shown the wet on it, wouldn't it? With that rain. Unless, of course, he'd put on an overcoat—and, well, *that* would have made no difference."

Westerham looked keenly at the Chief Constable, puffing away at his pipe as he did so. Then he took the pipe from his lips and said,

"Do you know who this fellow with the brown suit is, then, Major?"

"Yes—I do," replied the other, shortly.

"Oh!" exclaimed Westerham, arching his eyebrows. And there was considerable expression in the monosyllable.

"There's no reason why I shouldn't tell you this much," went on the Major, after a little reflection, "we're speaking in confidence—and, after all, you and I found poor Nayland's body —well—he's from South America."

"Oh—*is* he?" And, again, there was much intonation in the few words.

To this Major Challow made no reply. And then Westerham added,

"Another hypothesis—you think?"

"Perhaps," replied the Major curtly.

"Rather fits in with Garcia's story, doesn't it?" asked Westerham, drily.

But the Major said nothing in reply.

"May I ask a question?" went on Westerham.

"What?"

"I did put it to Ringwood—perhaps I ought not to have done so. But he would not answer it. Very likely you won't, either, Major. But it's this. Were any finger prints found on the handle of the knife?"

Major Challow got up to go,

"I don't know that I ought to say anything about that, padre," he replied, "But I'll tell you what. I should rather like to get the thumb print of that fellow in the brown suit, what! Now I must get hold of my wife and be off."

Westerham nodded. But he had no time to think of developments just then, the fete claimed his attention. As soon as he came out again into the garden he found plenty to do. Presently he strolled into the meadow where the "side shows" were in evidence, stood for a few minutes watching a group of farmers bowling for the pig, was enveigled into trying his skill at "hoop-la," but drew a blank, and laughingly passed on. A little group was gathered by the dart throwing competition, and he looked on while James Burt, the butler at "The Pleasaunce," won three packets of cigarettes in succession.

"You're in luck, Burt," he said.

"I am, sir," replied the butler, touching his hat with a dignified respectfulness, "but they're not much use to me. Here, take them back," he said, to the man who was overlooking the competition, "they'll do again, and it's all for a good cause."

The Vicar thanked him, and strolled on, parting with six pence to an intriguing young lady who coaxed him to pay that sum for a numbered peg to put in the space of ground allotted to the "treasure hunt."

Then he came to the palmist's tent. The flap was open, and Diana was sitting there alone. She caught sight of him.

"Won't you come in, my pretty gentleman, and let the gipsy tell your fortune?"

He turned and looked at her.

"I haven't come into it yet," he said, with a laugh.

"Perhaps I may help you!" she pleaded.

"Perhaps you *will!*" he replied. The brown stain on her face hid the warm blush she felt stealing over it—for there came to her a sudden meaning in his emphasis.

"Do come in," she repeated, "and show me your hand."

He went inside the tent, and she let down the flap. Then he took the seat opposite to her—a little table in between them.

"Now then," he said, keeping up the fiction, "does the gipsy really understand her art—or is she going to give me a hectic character?"

"Let the pretty gentleman give the poor gipsy a piece of silver to cross his hand with, and then she'll tell him."

He produced half a crown and held his hand to her across the table. She took it, and began to examine the lines on it.

It was the usual kind of thing, and the girl really knew something about her subject, though, as is customary on such occasions, a personal knowledge of the owner of the hand was a considerable help. She pattered away about the "line of life," the "line of the heart," the "plain of Mars," and so forth. And she told him very palpable truths, with the usual spice of flattery in them, that he had a strong will, a logical mind, that he was possessed of a strict regard for the truth, had a keen sense of humour—it always pleases the most obtuse person to say that, though in Westerham's case it was true—was a most observant person, and had a habit of doggedly getting to the root of things and overcoming obstacles.

This last remark set Westerham's mind straying far away from that tent interior—recalling his recent conversation with Major Challow and the mysterious man in brown. The latter loomed large in his thoughts, as he said to Diana,

"You've given me quite a nice character—but I suppose it's policy to magnify the good points, eh?"

She laughed,

"Oh, well—people like to be a little flattered, don't they?"

"What do you tell them when you find a really bad hand?" he went on, "if you really believe there's anything in it, you know."

Her eyes took on a graver light.

"I *do* think there's something in it. One or two people have puzzled me today—and I haven't liked to tell them all I saw."

"You'd be useful as a detective," he said, his mind still centering on the subject of the murder, "it's not a bad idea. The police have developed the science of finger prints for identification purposes, but I don't imagine they've brought palmistry—cheiromancy is the scientific term—into their observations, as a help to character study."

"What do you mean?" she asked, a little puzzled.

"Well, I was wondering what sort of a delineation you'd give on the hand of this fellow Garcia—whether it would help to find out if he spoke the truth. And I was wondering if—by the way," he broke off, suddenly, "there's a question I want to ask you. You've lived in this neighbourhood longer than I have, and you know the people. At that garden party the other day, did you notice a man with a small red moustache wearing a brown suit.

Do you know his name?"

Diana Garforth was still holding Westerham's hand lightly in hers. As he said the words her grip suddenly tightened, and an alarmed expression came into her eyes.

"Whatever makes you ask me that?" she replied, hurriedly, "no —I—I don't suppose I noticed any such person. There was such a crowd, wasn't there? Now—I haven't quite finished—will you spread out your fingers—yes—that's it. Oh, you know you've got a bit of a temper at times! Is that true?"

So she went on, hastily, rattling off her delineation, and not giving him any opportunity to interrupt. And when she had finished it was evident she was anxious to get rid of him.

"There are several people waiting to come in," she said, jumping up and raising the tent flap, "I hope you think you've had your money's worth."

Westerham went out, puzzled. For he was certain that Diana knew something about this mysterious man who, so Major Challow had told him, hailed from South America. Was it possible that—no, he couldn't believe anything wrong of Diana. But it worried him greatly.

Afterwards, Westerham said that he looked back to that fete in the Vicarage grounds as the day on which his mind first began to grasp a new idea in the Coppleswick mystery. He had turned his attention to the fete once more, with, however, the affair still in his sub-conscious mind. And presently he noticed something, quite casual in itself, which became imprinted on that sub-conscious mind of his. And what is once imprinted on that mind, psychologists tell us is registered there once for all.

CHAPTER 11

There alighted from the London train at the little station of Coppleswick, a young man wearing a fashionably cut suit with double breasted jacket, and a soft hat. He was a good looking fellow, but there were dark rims under his eyes and he gave the appearance of one who had either passed through some trouble, or had been leading a dissipated life.

He evidently knew the locality, for as soon as he was clear of the station precincts he left the main road, getting over a stile, and making his way by a foot-path across the fields. And the direction in which he was walking was that of Beechcroft.

When he arrived at the house he still showed that he was no stranger. He just opened the front door and walked in without knocking. He looked inside the drawing room, but there was no one there, then he made his way to a small room at the back of the house, known as the "morning room," but used at all hours of the day, more especially by Diana.

Diana herself was there, writing. She looked up quickly as the door opened, and gave a start of surprise.

"Hullo, Di, old girl. How goes it?"

"Harvey!" she exclaimed, jumping up from her seat, "why—you—" and she came towards him. He kissed her.

"Bit of a surprise, eh? Didn't expect me? I say, I suppose the governor's not in, is he?"

"No, he's in London. But what—"

"That's all right," he broke in, "I'd calculated on that. Last time I was here he wasn't exactly hospitable."

He threw himself into an easy chair and lighted a cigarette.

"Was he, Di?" he went on.

"Can you wonder, Harvey?" said the girl, as she sat down in a chair, facing him, "after all the trouble you gave him—and the money?"

"Oh, don't pile it on," he retorted, "I daresay I did annoy him a bit. But he needn't have cut up so beastly rough. Hang it all."

And he shrugged his shoulders.

"Where have you been all this time?" asked Diana, presently, "You've never written—not even to me."

"Sorry. I got out of the way of writing—and I'd got other things to think about. Where have I been? Oh, all over the shop. Abroad, most of the time."

"And what have you been doing?" and she looked at him earnestly.

"Oh, that's another story. I've had infernally bad luck. Pretty rotten, I can tell you. But I'm not going to talk about that. There's something I've come to see you about, Di. I'd hoped I should find you alone."

"Look here, Harvey," replied the girl, "I daresay I can guess what it is. But I *can't* help you any more. I've only got my allowance from Daddy, and I gave you all I had when you were here last. I even over-drew my account at the bank to do it, and I've only just got square again."

"It was topping of you, old girl," said Harvey, "but don't you get peeved. I've not come to ask you for anything. Fact of the matter is," and he laughed, shortly, "I'm a good boy, just at present. Turned over a jolly old—no—new leaf, and all that sort of thing, don't you know?"

"Oh, Harvey—you're not joking?" and she leaned forward, eagerly.

"The truth, the whole truth, and nothing but the truth. That's about it, Di. The only thing is, can I keep it up. Honestly, I meant to. I've been a hectic fool, and all that sort of thing—but, just now, I've tumbled into a job. And I want to stick it."

"What is it, Harvey?"

He laughed once more.

"Oh, no great shakes. Not the sort of thing the governor would care for, I fancy. I'm working in a garage, Di. And this is my half day off."

"In a garage?"

"Yes,—run by a pal of mine, an ex-service Johnny with D.S.O. after his name. Must do *something*, these times, you know. He knew I was down, and nearly out—that's another story—so he offered me a show. Lucky for me I know something about cars. I'm in the office—book-keeping, and so on—and help in the sales. Three quid a week and commission and a chance of more if things hum."

"Oh, I *am* glad, dear. I do hope you'll stick to it. It's better than —than—"

"Out with it, old girl—better than doing nothing—or the other thing. Yes—well," and he looked uncomfortable, "You see—I've—had a bit of a fright."

He blurted this out. She looked at him, curiously.

"Yes?" she asked.

"You won't say anything to the governor about it? Promise!"

"No—if you don't want me to."

"I don't. He wouldn't understand. I very nearly got into serious trouble, you see, Di."

"How?"

"Oh, well, I'm not going to tell even you all about it. But I got mixed up with some devilish shady Johnnies, one in particular —when I was coming home from abroad. He'd got something on me and there'd have been a deuce of a lot of trouble if it had come out. Thank the Lord it hasn't, though."

"What was it?"

"Oh, something I'd signed—it was only a matter of fifty quid, but this fellow got to know something—something about it, you see."

"I don't quite see," she replied, quietly, "wasn't it—well— *straight*, Harvey?"

He flushed and looked down.

"Oh, well," he said, "I don't want to talk about it, only this chap held it over me. He wanted a jolly sight more than fifty quid for it, and I was stony broke. But it's all right now," he added, "I've got it back—and destroyed it—you bet!"

"How did you get it back?" she asked.

"That's more than I can tell you, Di. I don't know."

"You don't *know?*"

"Fact! It came by post. I've been in London for the last five months—in lodgings."

"At—yes—where?"

"Oh, Notting Hill. And the other morning a registered letter came and I signed for it. The envelope was directed in block capitals—and inside was this beastly thing—nothing else."

"You're sure it *was* the—the thing?" she asked, hastily.

"Rather. No mistaking it."

A little sigh, as of relief, escaped her.

"Oh, I *am* so glad. Then it's all right now?"

"Yes, it's all right now, Di. But I tell you I went through hell. That's what I meant when I said I'd had a fright. It's sobered me, old dear."

"And—this man. Have you seen him since?"

"No. Never set eyes on him. I believe he's cleared out."

"And you haven't any idea why it—why he sent it back to you?"

"Not the slightest. It's an absolute mystery. But, at any rate, I'm clear now."

"He—this man—has got nothing more against you? You're sure?"

"Certain. I tell you, I can breathe freely now—and that's more than I was doing a couple of weeks ago. I don't want to talk about it any more, Di—except to say I've had my lesson. But I want you to do something for me. I'm sure you will."

"Of course. If I can. What is it?"

She was smiling a happy smile as she looked at him. For three or four years this brother of hers had been a great anxiety. He was well educated, had taken, his degree at Oxford, and his father had hoped that he would have been called to the Bar. But he had gone off at a tangent, refusing to settle down to anything,

123

running into debt, and, from time to time, returning home to get things cleared, always with the promise of making a fresh start. At last his father's patience, to say nothing of his purse, had been tried to the limit. He had given Harvey a sum of money and told him plainly that he did not wish to see him again until he could give a satisfactory account of himself. Till then, he forbade him the house.

And then, after this, he had sponged on his sister more than once. She had not dared to tell her father, knowing how furious he would be, but she had helped him, as she had said, out of her allowance.

At last, however, things seemed to have taken a turn for the better—if what he had told her about sticking to his job was true.

"What is it you want me to do?" she repeated.

"Just to try to get me right with dad," he replied, "I want you to tell him you've seen me—you can say I've been here, if you like, and that I really mean to make a jolly good try of it. You'll do that, won't you, Di?"

"Why, of course I will. Daddy will be tremendously pleased—he's felt things keenly all these months, though he hasn't said very much. But *I* know! But why not see him yourself?"

"No—not till I've made good. I want him to know I'm trying, that's all. I've got a bit of pride left still, thank goodness, and when I *do* see him I want to be independent—to prove to him that I haven't come to ask him for anything. And, Di, for the Lord's sake don't you say a word to him about what I've told you. That's between you and me. Swear you won't!"

"No—I won't say anything, Harvey. Really, you know, you haven't told me exactly what it was."

"And I probably shan't, either. I want to forget it. Look here, you must write me a line and tell me how the governor takes things. I'll give you my address. Hullo—still the same old book, I see."

On the table, amid her writing materials, was lying a little note book, one of those handy compendiums alphabetically arranged for names and addresses. She had used it for years, and

Harvey, recognising it, put out his hand to take it.

"I'll write it down," he said.

But before he could touch the little address book she had snatched it off the table with a quick motion.

"I'll do it myself," she said, a little confusedly.

"Oh, all serene—I don't want to see your secrets," he said, with a laugh, "Go ahead, then—27 Albion Street, Notting Hill—got it?"

She nodded as she wrote it down. But anyone looking over her shoulder at the book, open at the letter "H," would have been surprised to see that the address was already there!

"I say," exclaimed Harvey, presently, as they chatted together, "you've had some excitement down here over that murder case, by Jove! I've read about it in the papers, of course. Did you know this man, Nayland?"

"Why, yes. I was at the garden party where it happened. Horrible, wasn't it?"

"Pretty beastly, yes. Did you see this fellow who was disguised as a bandsman?"

"Yes, I did. But I didn't notice him particularly, you know."

"I suppose it's pretty certain he did it, eh?"

Diana paused for a moment or two, and then said,

"Daddy doesn't feel at all sure about it. You know how interested he always gets in a crime of this kind? Well, he's talked a lot about it, and he's very much inclined to believe this man Garcia's explanation—all that he said at the inquest, you know."

"Is he, by Jove! Then he thinks someone else did it?"

She nodded.

"But who else could have done it?"

A troubled look came into her eyes; her cheeks paled a little.

"How should I know?" she said, "There were so many people there."

He looked at his watch,

"Oh, well," he said, "Garcia's sure to be committed for trial and then I daresay a lot more will come out—the police have a habit of keeping things up their sleeves till they're ready. I must be off now. There's a train back to London I want to catch."

"I'll walk with you to the station," she said, "just give me a minute to put my hat on."

Before she left the room, however, she was careful to put her writing materials, the little address book among them, into the table drawer—which she locked. In five minutes the two were walking together across the fields to the station.

The train which Harvey Garforth intended to take was a slow one to London, stopping at every station, and starting from Sydbury. When it drew up at the platform at Coppleswick a solitary passenger got out. Diana, who was saying goodbye to her brother, did not notice him at the moment, but when the train had gone, and she was on the point of leaving the station, he came up to her, raising his hat as he did so. It was Detective Sergeant Ringwood.

"I beg your pardon," he said, "but I believe I am speaking to Miss Garforth?"

"Yes—I am Miss Garforth," replied Diana, wondering a little who he was and what he wanted.

"I was on my way to see you," he went on.

"Yes?" she asked.

"I am in the police force, Miss Garforth," he replied, "my name is Ringwood. And there is just a little matter I wanted to ask you about—privately."

She bit her lip, involuntarily. She had been prepared for this, the Vicar had told her that it was likely that the police might wish to interview her about that handkerchief. But, now that it had come she was momentarily taken aback. And yet, like a flash, she realised that this man would make a study of the attitude in which she received any question he might put to her, as well as her answers to them. She made a desperate effort to appear only a little bit surprised, as any one might be, in a casual sort of way.

"To ask me some questions?" she said, frowning a little, "But whatever are they about?"

He did not answer this. Instead he remarked,

"Were you walking back home, Miss Garforth?"

"Yes—I was."

"Then would you allow me to go part of the way with you? It would save me the trouble of going to your house"—and he darted a keen glance at her—"and I can say all I want to."

"Very well," she replied, "I was going across the fields. Will that suit you?"

"Quite. We are not likely to be disturbed there."

Walking along the road, and until they reached the stile leading into the field path, Ringwood made ordinary remarks about the weather. But as soon as they were in the field he began.

"I am investigating the murder of Mr Nayland," he said, "and please don't be alarmed, Miss Garforth."

"Why should I be alarmed?" she asked, coldly.

"Quite so. We policemen, you know," and he spoke very suavely, "are obliged to enquire into all sorts of things in a case like this, which, really, may have nothing to do with it at all. But we have to be satisfied, and that, for two main reasons. We have no wish that the innocent should suffer, but we *do* want to bring the guilty to justice."

"I understand," she replied, "and, of course, that is very natural. Yes?"

"Well, now," he went on, "I want you first of all, if you will, Miss Garforth, to tell me if this is your handkerchief?" and he drew the article in question out of his pocket and gave it to her.

"Yes," she said, at once, "it is. What made you think so? It has only my initials on it—not my name."

"You must give us credit for a little ordinary common sense," he replied, with a smile, "I have a list of all the guests who were at the garden party at 'The Pleasaunce,' and you were the only lady present with those initials."

"Oh," she said, at once, "then you found it there, Mr Ringwood?"

"Yes—I did," he replied, "had you missed it?"

"Why, naturally—but a handkerchief isn't of much consequence, and I didn't bother about it."

"I found it," he went on, ignoring what she had said, "just after the murder was committed—when I came on the scene. It was lying in the wood beyond the garden—not on the path, but right in among the trees, some little distance away from the path."

"Yes," she said, as nonchalantly as possible, "I suppose I must have dropped it there. Quite a number of people went into the wood that day—after tea."

Ringwood, who had the details and times of that garden party accurately in his mind, at once went on, and said,

"Yes, I quite understand that, and I don't want to suggest for a moment that I think there was anything suspicious in your dropping the handkerchief there. But I do want to know whether you were in the wood when the concert was taking place in the hall—any time, say, from half past five onwards."

"But what can that have to do with it?" she asked.

"You will see in a moment, Miss Garforth. Do you mind telling me what time you were there?"

"Yes," she replied, after a moment's reflection, in which she determined to anticipate the question she thought he would put next, "of course I will tell you. I was in the wood while the concert was going on. But, if you imagine because of this that I saw anything, let me say at once that I didn't. I never returned to the house at all. I was on my way home through that wood. And I never saw either Mr Nayland or the man Garcia."

"Quite so," replied the detective, "I didn't think you did, for a moment, because I always felt sure if you had seen them you would have said something about it. And that's why, to begin with, I didn't bother you. But circumstances have changed since then, and I want a little more information. Miss Garforth, did you see anyone else in that wood when you were there?"

"Isn't that rather an absurd question? There were so many people at the garden party—and—"

"Yes, I know," he interrupted, "But just then it was raining hard and the guests were indoors. Come, Miss Garforth, this is in the interests of justice. You must see that. If there was anyone else in that wood between say half past five, or a little later, and six o'clock, and you saw him, it is your plain duty to tell me."

"I understand," she replied, in a low voice, "very well then—I did see someone. But I am sure it had nothing to do with the murder."

A gleam of satisfaction momentarily shone in the detective's eyes.

"One of the guests, I suppose?" he questioned, apparently carelessly.

"Someone who was at the garden party. Yes."

"You were with him?"

"Ye-es. I was."

"Oh!"

It had been more or less a chance shot on the part of the detective; though, as he had discovered the handkerchief away from the path, he had shrewdly guessed that Diana had gone aside with some other person. In his mind he had conjected that this person might have been her lover, and he had been, really, prepared for no further disclosure, though he wanted to make certain. But the fact that she had evaded his direct question as to whether the person with whom she had been in the wood was an actual guest, put him on the qui vive at once.

"Who was he?" he asked abruptly.

"That is my business," she retorted.

"And mine, too," he said, quietly, "I am sorry I must push the question, Miss Garforth. May I suggest that he was wearing a brown suit of clothes and a billy cock hat, and that he had a small, red moustache?"

They were walking, slowly, across the fields. She stopped short and turned to him.

"What makes you ask me that?"

He smiled.

"You've already told me," he replied, "you gave me to understand that although he was at the garden party he was not one of the invited guests. And we happen to have found out that there *was* a man there who came uninvited. Also, we not only know how he was dressed, but who he was."

"Then," replied Diana, emphatically, "you know a great deal more about him that I do. For *I* don't know who he was."

"Oh—but you were with him?"

"Yes."

"May I not suggest," he said, quietly, "that it's a little bit queer that you and he should be alone together in that wood, and that all the time he was a perfect stranger to you?"

"Of course it's queer, Mr Ringwood, I know. But it's absolutely true, though I cannot explain it to you. It was a private matter between him and me. I don't suppose he even knew Mr Nayland, and he certainly didn't come there to murder him. And I don't see what all this has to do with the case at all, or with the man you've got—Garcia."

The detective nodded, sympathetically. He knew exactly how far he wanted to go, and he still had a notion that it might have been a case of a clandestine lover. He was sorry for Diana, but he had to get one more bit of information before he had finished with her.

"I'm not suggesting that he had anything to do with the murder, Miss Garforth," he went on, soothingly, "and I'm sure *you* hadn't. But I want you to tell me if I am right in my supposition. You were with this man at the further end of the wood, near the gate which leads into the lane at the back of it? Very well. And you say you went out at that gate? Quite so. What did he do?"

"The last I saw of him—he was going back to 'The Pleasaunce' by the path leading through the wood."

"And the time?"

She hesitated.

"The church clock struck six just after I got out into the lane."

The detective's eyes flashed in triumph. He had found the exact information he wanted.

"I'm most grateful to you, Miss Garforth," he said, "And I'm very sorry to have troubled you. But it *is* important."

"I've told you all I can," said the girl, "but the rest is a private matter, I assure you. But why have you asked me all this? Is anything going to happen about it—in public, I mean?"

Ringwood noticed the genuine distress and consternation showed by the girl.

"I can't tell you yet, Miss Garforth," he said, "but I promise to let you know at once if we find you will be wanted as a witness later on."

"A witness!" she exclaimed, "oh, but why?"

"You really mustn't be alarmed. If it comes to that all you will have to do is to say exactly what you have told me—there's no blame in anyway attached to you."

"But—but—will they cross question me?"

He nodded.

"You must expect that, I'm afraid."

"And ask me—*why* I was with this man? What he wanted?"

"I think that's obvious."

"But—you don't understand. I *can't* tell them. Is it really necessary?"

"Look here, Miss Garforth," he said, kindly, "I've only been doing my duty. I'm bound to find out all I can, and you're morally bound to tell all you know. And that's where I can't offer to help you—because you're keeping something back from me. But you talk it over with your father. Mr Garforth knows a great deal more than I do about witnesses, and, of course he'll help you. I'm sure when you've done that you'll find it will all be quite simple."

Talk it over with her father! That was the one thing Diana wanted to avoid. But she felt she *must* confide in someone, for she was at her wit's end.

CHAPTER 12

It was with a great deal of satisfaction that Mr Garforth listened that evening to the story which Diana had to tell him about her brother, though he did not make many comments at the time. There had been more than one occasion when Harvey had made promises tending to reformation, and his father was still a little sceptical. Of course Diana kept her promise and said nothing about the other affair.

"I'm delighted to hear all this," remarked Mr Garforth, "and I hope it's the beginning of better things. Do you know his address, Di?"

"Yes,—I've got it here."

"Very well, I shall write to him at once."

"You won't be too severe, Daddy dear?" she asked, "I'm sure he means to try hard."

"No, I won't be unmerciful in any way. But I want him to be put to the test a little. I shall tell him he may come and spend the weekend here—next month—if he's still in the same job. And then we can talk matters over. I've always promised to help him if he's steady and sticks to a thing, and I will. But I want him to fend for himself a little longer before we put things quite on the old basis.

"Oh," he went on presently, "I knew there was something I wanted to say to you, Di. You've often said you'd like to go to a big city dinner, eh?"

"Oh, rather, Daddy."

"Well, I've had an invitation today to one—the Drapers' Company. It's their ladies night, and the invitation includes one.

So I'm going to take you."

"Oh, Daddy, how perfectly ripping!"

He laughed.

"I think you'll enjoy it," he said "not only the actual dinner, I mean, but they're sure to have a first-rate concert or some other form of entertainment. And it's a smart affair, you know. I want you to dress up to it—and I'd like you to wear your pearl necklace."

He did not notice the sudden start she gave, as she put down her half raised glass on the table again—they were at dinner.

"Oh, Daddy," she said, hesitating a little, "I don't think I can. You see my best frock is the mauve one, with those sparkly brilliants on it—and pearls wouldn't go with it at all. They'd simply clash horridly."

"Wear your black velvet frock. There's nothing like it to show up pearls."

"Oh, but—it's out of fashion; *quite*. I *couldn't*."

Her father laughed at her, but then said, quite seriously,

"Really, I want you to wear that necklace, Di. It suits you. Don't you think I want to feel a little proud of my daughter?"

"Yes, I know. And it's frightfully nice of you to say so, Daddy, but—"

"Well" he broke in "You know what I wish. I shall be running into Sydbury on Saturday, and I'll get them out of the bank for you."

"Oh, don't do that," she began, hastily, but went on, "I mean— I expect they'll have to be restrung. I can run in tomorrow, you know. There's a Sydbury jeweller could do it, if it wants doing. Only—all the same—I'd rather wear my lilac frock. It's just a dinky one—and up to date."

He shrugged his shoulders, just a wee bit annoyed by her persistence.

"Get them out of the bank tomorrow, and have them re-strung, at all events," he said, "If you don't, *I* shall—on Saturday."

If anything was wanting to help her to the solution of an idea she had had in her mind ever since her interview with the detective it was this. And, before the evening was over, she had made her decision. The next morning, immediately after her father had started for London, or, rather, as soon as the chauffeur had brought back the car from the station, she jumped into it and drove at once to Coppleswick Vicarage.

Westerham was working at his desk when Diana was shown into the study. For the maid had assumed that this early visitor was one of the constant little stream who came to see the Vicar on matters connected with the parish, and he always received such amid his business surroundings. He sprang to his feet, a smile on his face, and shook hands with her cordially. His desk was covered with accounts and papers relating to the fete, and she gladly made this a first excuse for her call.

"I've got a little more money from my palmistry affair," she explained, "and I thought you'd like to have it."

"Thanks," he said, "I shall be glad to get the thing squared up. We've done very well, you know—quite a tidy sum."

"I'm so glad. And," she went on presently, "there's something else, you see . . . I want to consult you, if I may?"

"Why, of course."

"I'm most frightfully worried, Mr Westerham. I've had a visit from the police—about that handkerchief. You were quite right when you said they'd probably come to me."

He was grave in a moment.

"Yes," he answered, "I thought they would. Was it Detective Sergeant Ringwood?"

She nodded.

"And he asked you a lot of questions?""

"Oh, he was dreadful! Quite nice, all the time, you know. But he seemed to drag things out of me. Things I thought I could keep to myself—and, I don't quite know what to do. You said I might ask your help if I wanted it."

"I'm so glad you've come. Of course I'll help you, if I can. It's bothered me frightfully at times, and I've been wishing all along that I could be of some use."

She looked up at him gratefully and met his steadfast gaze.

And she knew she could trust this man.

"May I tell you, to begin with, all that this detective got out of me?"

"Please do. I won't interrupt till you've finished."

He listened attentively as she told her story—plainly and vividly.

"Yes," he said, slowly, when she had done, "it's partly what I'd guessed myself. I felt certain you knew something about this fellow in brown—from your manner at the fete, when I mentioned him. Now, what did Sergeant Ringwood say when you told him all this?"

"He said I might have to give evidence. But I can't see why."

"I'll tell you. I'm pretty well sure the police have their doubts about Manoel Garcia, though, of course, they're bound to keep him in custody just now. I think, somehow, they'll apply for a further remand—that means putting off his trial, you know. And I also think they're after this fellow in brown. Well, don't you see, you'd be a very important witness. You'd have to say exactly where you saw him last—and the time."

Diana had taken off her gloves, and sat, nervously twisting them in her fingers.

"Ye-es. I see," she said slowly.

"And didn't Ringwood give you any advice?"

"Yes. He did. And that's just what is worrying me."

"What was it?"

"He advised me to talk it over with Daddy."

"Well," replied Westerham, quietly, "isn't that the very best thing you can do?"

She shook her head.

"I *can't*," she murmured.

"But why not?"

"Because—because. Oh, let me say something first. Do you think this man—the one in brown—committed the murder?"

"I can't say—how *can* I?"

"I'm sure he didn't."

He nodded.

"I suppose you've a reason for saying so, but then I don't know what that reason is."

"Well, I'm going to tell you. That's where I want your help," she said.

He leaned forward and laid his hand lightly on one of hers,

"Before you tell me anything," he said, "I want you to believe that never for a moment have I thought you were mixed up in this horrible affair. I've been sorely puzzled, I admit—but not *that!*"

"You're awfully good to me," she replied, in a low voice, trembling a little.

"And I also want to say that if you'd rather not tell me any more I shan't ask you to."

She looked up at him.

"But I *must*. I must tell someone. And I'd rather it was you than anyone else."

"Thank you," he said quietly. "Well, then?"

"I think you've met my brother, Harvey?" she began.

"Yes—last year. I remember,"

"You probably know he's been a great trouble to us? I know it's talked about."

"I don't listen to gossip if I can avoid it—but I couldn't help it once or twice. Yes, I've thought that."

"He's been frightfully wild. He wouldn't settle down to anything. And he got into debt several times. Daddy paid his debts at first, and then there came a time when there was an awful row between them. My father has a temper when it's roused. And Harvey was forbidden the house: that was ten months ago. Daddy said he was not to come back to it till he could show he'd turned over a new leaf. And all this time we've heard nothing of him."

Westerham nodded sympathetically, but said nothing. He waited a few moments, and Diana went on.

"Well, it was at that garden party—just before tea. I was standing in the corner of the lawn, alone at the moment. I'd just been talking to Mrs Leigh-Hulcott. And, suddenly, this man in brown came up to me and took off his hat. I hadn't the slightest idea who he was, but naturally thought he was one of the guests. You remember what a crowd of people were there. He began by saying 'Miss Garforth, I believe?' Of course I said 'Yes,' and expected him to tell me who he was, and make the usual inane remarks about the weather. So you may guess how surprised I was when he went on, at once, to say he was a friend of Harvey's, and that he'd come from London that afternoon on purpose to see me. I said I supposed he knew I was going to be at the garden party—I couldn't think of anything else to say at the moment. And then he laughed and told me an extraordinary story. He spoke with a touch of an Irish accent, and his voice was sort of silky—you know. Well, he said he had called at our house that afternoon and the maid had told him I'd gone to the Nayland's garden party, that he'd asked if it was a big party, and the maid had said she thought it was. 'So,' he went on, 'I followed you here. I guessed if it was going to be a crowd I could easily slip in, and I *have*.' 'But *why*?' I asked."

"What did he say to that?"

"He laughed again. 'I haven't any time to waste,' he answered, 'that's why I took this chance of seeing you. I motored down, and my car's outside where they're parking them. Now, look here, I've got to see you alone—away from all these folks. It's about your brother, and it's a serious matter. He's in danger of going to prison and it's up to you to stop that. No more now. When will you meet me?'"

"You can imagine how I felt, can't you? I tried to pull myself together a bit, and I told him I'd be in the wood behind the garden when the glee concert was going on. I thought that would be the best time, as the others would not be likely to notice if I slipped away. Of course I thought the concert would be held on the lawn, but when I knew it was to be in the house, and when it came on to rain, I was glad, because I thought there'd be less chance of being seen. Well, I slipped off soon after the concert had begun, and there he was—waiting in the path in the wood. We turned aside so as to be under shelter."

"What did he want?"

She shuddered.

"I very soon found out; it was blackmail!"

"Blackmail?"

"Yes. He said he'd met Harvey on a boat coming over from Rio de Janeiro—we didn't even know he'd been abroad. And I suppose they played cards, and Harvey lost. The end of it seemed to be that Harvey hadn't enough money to pay, and had given him a cheque—for fifty pounds. That was after his return, in London. And—and—" Diana's face paled as she looked down and hesitated, "Harvey hadn't signed it with his own name—but with father's."

"Forgery!"

She nodded.

"Wasn't it dreadful?" she asked.

"You poor girl," he exclaimed, pityingly, "How I wish I'd been there."

She shook her head.

"You couldn't have helped me."

"I should have asked him to prove his story, to begin with."

"He did. He showed me the cheque. There was no doubt about it."

"Well, and then?"

"You can guess, can't you? He was brutally frank about it. He gave me the choice of buying that cheque from him for five hundred pounds, or either he would present it at the bank and let things take their course, or go to my father with it. 'I haven't made up my mind which,' he said, 'I might drive a bargain with your father, but either of the two courses would ruin your brother.' What was I to do?"

"Yes, I see," answered Westerham, "He was an absolute brute—and a clever one, too. That's why he trailed on you, instead of on your father."

"How?"

"Well, of course it's quite natural that you couldn't see it at the time, but if he *had* gone to your father, Mr Garforth had only to tell him to present the cheque and give instructions to the bank to pay it, and *this* rascal wouldn't have much more out of it than its face value. He knew that very well, and that's why he bullied you."

"But there was always Harvey's disgrace?"

"Yes, I know. And you wanted to save him, out of pure goodness of heart. Well, what did he say next?"

"That he'd give me time to raise the money, for I told him I hadn't got it. He only laughed, and said no doubt I'd some articles of jewelry I could raise it on, that first put the idea into my head—but, I'll tell you. He said if I would buy that cheque he'd be at Charing Cross station, under the clock, at three in the afternoon of the following Monday. And that that was the last chance. Then he said he must be getting back to London, and we parted. The last I saw of him, as I told the Detective Sergeant Ringwood, was when he was going back along the path through the wood—I went out into the lane, and it was just then that the clock struck six."

"And it was just then that Nayland must have had that knife stuck into him. That's the point, you see. But we'll come to that presently. Did you raise the money?"

She nodded.

"You saw me beginning to do it—at the Sydbury Bank. I was getting a case that contained some bits of jewelry, a pearl necklace among them—the most valuable thing I possessed. I went straight up to London, and got a loan on it."

"You didn't sell it outright?"

"No. A girl friend of mine got into a bother about losses at bridge, and she had told me how she raised money on some bracelets and rings. I had remembered the place she went to —luckily. They lent me five hundred pounds on the pearls—in notes. This man had said I must pay him in cash and not by cheque. Then I went to Charing Cross station. He was there, and he gave me the cheque."

"Did he say anything about the murder?" asked Westerham, leaning forward.

"Not a word."

"Umph! Evidently, even if he did it, he didn't think he was suspected. But of course he'd read all about the hue and cry after the bandsman. Yes?"

"Well, the next thing to do was to get the cheque back to Harvey. At first I'd thought I would take it to him, so I asked this man for his address. He gave it to me. Then I changed my mind. You see I didn't really want Harvey to know that I'd got it back. So I bought an envelope, wrote the address in printed letters on it, put the cheque inside, and posted it—by registered post."

"Oh, but I say," exclaimed Westerham, "that was an awful risk. This fellow may not have given you the correct address—it may only have been a blind to get it back into his own hands."

"I thought of that, afterwards," said Diana, "and it gave me a pretty bad time. But it's all right. Harvey's been here since—and told me."

And she explained how her brother had merely hinted at some compromising document.

"And, you see," she added, "I promised him faithfully I wouldn't tell Daddy about it. And now, not only does this detective threaten me with a cross examination, when it might all come out, but my father wants me to wear those pearls at a city dinner he's taking me to next week, and he says he'll go to Sydbury and ask for them at the bank on Saturday—if I haven't taken them out before. Oh, what am I to do?"

"Well, in the first place, leave off worrying," he said, laying his hand on hers again, "You've done nothing to be ashamed of—quite the contrary. You've been awfully brave and plucky. If it's necessary I'll get these pearls out of pawn for you—I'd willingly advance the money—"

"I couldn't—oh, I couldn't take it!"

"Why not? it would only be a loan. But I don't think it's the best way out. It means keeping up the deception. If you *have* to give evidence it would have to come out—more or less. But you needn't say the thing this fellow sold you was a cheque forged by your brother. Don't you see? All that is necessary is to say it was an incriminating document, and stick to that."

She looked at him a little more hopefully.

"You really think that?" she asked.

"I do. But your father will have to know."

"But I can't tell him."

"No. You've promised that. Well, you can keep your promise. Your brother will have to tell him."

"But—"

"No 'buts,' please. Of course he will. I'm going to see this brother of yours and just tell him what you've done. Oh yes, you must let me do that! It's only fair. And if he's got any grit of course he'll tell your father—and—don't you see—it's best that your father should know it from him—if there's the slightest chance of it's coming out—isn't it?"

"Ye-es, I suppose it is," she admitted, "You're most awfully good."

"Not a bit. You've come to me to help you out and I'm going to see the thing through. It'll be all right, *really!* Only there's one more thing I want you to let me do. It may seem rather horrid at first, but I think it's a good move."

"What is it?"

"Well, I know Major Challow pretty intimately. And though he's a trifle pompous, he's a decent chap at heart. By this time he probably knows all you told Detective Sergeant Ringwood. But I want you to let me tell him the whole story—in absolute confidence. 'Without prejudice' as your father would call it."

"But I don't quite see why?"

"It's this way. It would give him a grip on the case which, in pure justice, he ought to have. I believe he's after this fellow in the brown suit. You say Ringwood told you the police know who he is. Very well then, it's more than probable that they'll arrest him. Let the Chief Constable have the truth to begin with. I'm sure its best. After all," he added, very gravely, "it's the duty of a citizen to help the police in a murder case. And we all want to find the guilty man—if they haven't found him already, and there seems to be a doubt about it."

"Do you think—then—after all—that the man I met in the wood did it?"

"I told you just now. I don't know. But I think he'll have to explain his movements. And if the police get him, and his story tallies with yours, and the Chief Constable knows the truth beforehand, why, it *may* mean that you wouldn't have to give evidence at all. Anyhow, I should like to tell him—if you'll let me?"

"Very well," said Diana, "I know whatever you do will be wise. I don't know how to thank you enough for your kindness and I can't tell you how you've relieved my mind."

She was preparing to go, but he said,

"I want your brother's address, you know—and the garage where he's working, if you've got it."

"Oh, yes."

They were both standing now, beside his desk. He gave her a pen and she bent down to write the address, Westerham looking over her shoulder as she did so. She turned her head when she had finished and met his gaze. And there was something in his expression which brought the colour rushing to her cheeks.

"You've been frightfully kind," she murmured.

He laid his hand gently on her shoulder.

"Don't you see what a pleasure it is to me to help you?" he said, "I'd rather help you than any one else in the world. Don't you know why?"

"No," she faltered, though the light in her eyes belied the word.

"I was going to tell you soon—and I can't wait any longer. It's just because I love you, dear. I've loved you ever since I first saw you—and I've wondered—oh, I've wondered . . ."

"What?" she asked, softly.

"Whether you would love me!"

She looked up at him again, and he saw the answer in the smile that lit up her face, before she said,

"You needn't really have wondered."

His arm slipped round her and he drew her to him,

"Dearest," he said "will you make me very happy? Will you be

142

my wife?"

"Yes, dear," she whispered, and their lips sealed the promise.

*

It was a happy Diana that stepped into her car a little later. And a glint of mischief shone in her eyes as she said to Harry Westerham,

"Come and see Daddy soon—but you mustn't tell him that I came here and that you proposed to me in your study. It would make me out to be a frightfully forward girl, you know—but I'm glad—for every reason—that I *did* come!"

CHAPTER 13

The Coppleswick murder case had now reached that peculiar stage at which the newspapers, for want of any further definite information, hinted at "new and startling developments." But they had no idea what those developments were likely to be, for the police were exceedingly chary of letting out their secrets.

Major Challow held sundry consultations with his head officials. They realised that they were up against certain difficulties. They were by no means sure that there was sufficient evidence now to convict Manoel Garcia, but at the same time it would never do to set him at large. Further delay was necessary, and this was achieved in the usual routine manner. When Garcia was brought before the Sydbury magistrates for the second time the police called no witnesses, but only asked for another remand, which was granted. Westerham had expected to be called, but was not. The butler at "The Pleasaunce" also expected the summons, for, of course his evidence was important. He was the last person to see Nayland and Garcia in close conjunction. He had even gone so far as to inquire of the police whether he was expected; he was arranging, he said, with Miss Nayland for a week's holiday and naturally did not wish to be away when the summons came. But he was told he would not be wanted just yet.

Meanwhile Westerham had had his interview with the Chief Constable and told him Diana's story. The Major was sympathetic, indignant indeed, at the position in which the blackmailer had placed her.

"If she has to give evidence," he told Westerham, "you can tell her that it isn't at all necessary that the actual fact of the forged cheque should come out. I would even go so far as to talk it over with the counsel for the defense, for I'm sure no self-respecting barrister would wish to drag an outsider, like Harvey Garforth, through the mud in cross-examination. I'm glad you've told me, padre. It only confirms me in what we know about this fellow already."

"Who is he?" asked Westerham, bluntly.

"Ah, you mustn't ask me that," retorted the Major. "I'd rather not say."

But Westerham discovered the man's name the very same day. After his interview with Major Challow he took a train to London and sought out Harvey Garforth. As he had expected, the young man rose to the occasion at once, and promised to make a clean breast to his father. Then he told Westerham what he knew about the blackmailer.

"His name is O'Calligan," he said "I only know him from travelling with him on the boat, but I fancy he'd been mixed up in South American politics—secretary to the president of some potty little republic I think I heard. He's a gentlemanly beggar, but a thorough scoundrel. I could have forgiven him for going for me—I suppose I deserved it, but if I ever come across him again I'll let him know what I think of his bullying my sister—in more ways than one."

Westerham had not let Harvey know that he was aware that the latter had forged his father's name to a cheque, only referring to it as a "compromising document." He thought that was as far as it was necessary to go.

Meanwhile, Major Challow had visited the Home Office and had been put in possession of all which that astute department knew of O'Calligan. They sent him on to the Foreign Office, and he gained more details from the Assistant Secretary there. Don Gonzolez, of the State of San Miguel, was still occupying the somewhat precarious presidential chair of that turbulent little country. He was, so the Assistant Secretary said, no better and no worse than so many of his kind who dabble in the complicated politics of South American states—perhaps a little stronger than some of them, for, under his rule, San Miguel had quieted down, though there was always a chance of the opposing party executing a coup d'état, and putting Don Gonzolez up against a convenient wall as a target for a firing squad.

"Not that *we* want that to happen just now," went on the Assistant Secretary, "for an English Company has just obtained a concession to make a railway in San Miguel, and as this Gonzolez seems to keep things in pretty fair order it's as well that he should go on."

O'Calligan, he told the Major, was simply an adventurer, out for money, and not in the least caring how he came by it. He had acted as Secretary to Don Gonzolez both before and after the latter had obtained the presidency, and then attempted to feather his nest in a double way by selling important information to leaders of the late government who were conspiring to overthrow Gonzolez.

"He only escaped by the skin of his teeth," said the Secretary, "one of these nice johnnies jabbed at him with a knife—it's a pretty little habit some of them have out there—and he dodged it just in time, and ran the gauntlet. He wouldn't live many hours if he set foot in San Miguel again—and he knows it. That's why we handed his name over to the Home Office when we knew he was on his way here. We were right, you see. For I daresay if you can find out who Manoel Garcia really is you'll discover a link between the two. Well, he's in Paris now. You want him, I suppose?"

"I do," replied the Major, grimly.

"Question of an extradition warrant, of course. You're seeing about that?"

"I am," retorted the Chief Constable. "Now tell me. Scotland Yard mentioned an Englishman named Beech who was associated with O'Calligan. What do you know about his doings over the water, what?"

The Assistant Secretary consulted his data.

"Not very much," he said, "he was quite an inferior rascal,

apparently. Did some of O'Calligan's dirty work for him. No—he seems to have disappeared altogether. Question of a knife again, most likely. One thing we know about him, he seems to have quarrelled with O'Calligan before he disappeared."

"And a man named Ignace Valdez?" went on Major Challow, "any record about him?"

"No. Never heard of him. I know who you mean. I've read this case of yours in the paper, of course. I see you're advertising for him."

"Yes, we are," replied the Major, as he got up to go, "here, and in some of the Spanish papers, though it's a sort of forlorn hope. Garcia said, you know, he thought he was in Spain—but it's only a chance. Well—thank you very much, what?"

Manoel Garcia, kept under lock and key at Sydbury, was, of course, treated in the usual manner as a prisoner charged with a serious offence, but, according to the fairness of English law, technically considered innocent until that offence should be proved. The Chief Constable himself had explained to him that he was at liberty, under certain restrictions, to communicate with his friends, and that he could employ a lawyer to defend him. He had replied that he had no friends in England, but wished to write to a relative in South America, which, of course, he was allowed to do, under censorship. He had also said that he would like arrangements to be made by which he could draw on money that he had deposited in a London bank, that he knew no solicitor, but naturally wanted to consult one. In the end, a Sydbury lawyer named Keston, had visited him more than once in his cell.

Ernest Keston was a shrewd, sharp featured man of about five and forty with a practice that included a pretty close acquaintanceship with criminal law. It was true that he had never had to defend a capital charge, but those who knew him well said that he was quite capable of doing so. He was known in the district as "Silent Keston," an excellent nickname for one of his calling. The epithet "Silent" applied to that side of his profession where silence is generally golden, and to his habit of listening to a client without a word of interruption until that same client had stated his case from his own standpoint. In court Keston showed that he had a tongue—at times bitter and sarcastic.

What Garcia told him he kept to himself. Nor would he, by word or sign, intimate, even to his closest friends, what he really thought of the case he was undertaking.

Then came the surprise. But, when Major Challow thought it over afterwards he admitted to himself that he ought not to have been so joyfully surprised as he was, when, in the middle of luncheon one day, the maid brought in a visiting card with the intimation that the owner wished to see her master on important business, and that she had shown him into the library, telling him that the Major was engaged just then, but if he would wait would doubtless see him presently.

But the Major did not keep him waiting. Adjusting his monocle he read the name on the card, and incontinently rushed out of the room with an excited exclamation on his lips. In a few minutes he returned, with a curious question, addressed to his family in general.

"Here," he said, "do any of you know anyone in Sydbury who speaks Spanish?"

"Won't you finish your luncheon first, dear?" expostulated his wife.

"No, I won't, what!" he retorted, testily.

"Now then, can any of you tell me?" he repeated.

"Yes," said his eldest daughter, "I know. The cashier at the National Bank—he's lived in Spain."

"Sure?" asked her father.

"Quite sure. He took the Spanish and Commercial evening course in the Higher Education Syllabus last winter. I know, because Phyllis Mathers took up Spanish there."

In another minute Major Challow was at his telephone. He rang up the manager of the bank and asked for the loan of his cashier for half an hour, explaining that he wanted him to interpret a statement that a Spanish gentleman wished to make

—and would he please hold his tongue about it, and instruct his cashier to do likewise. Then he went back to the library, still holding in his hand the card which his maid had given him. And the name on this card, the name which had caused all this excitement, was,

"Señor Ignace Valdez."

In the library was seated a dapper little foreigner, well dressed and well groomed, dark, with a black moustache and small, pointed beard. And when the Major had entered the room he said, in broken English,

"You see I 'ave not at first known—Señor Nayland, was—'ow you say?"

"Was dead—murdered," explained the Major.

"Si, señor. Muy gracias. But I 'ave seen—in ze journals Espanol—and zen—my own name—you want 'im, eh?"

"I understand, Señor Valdez. You have seen my advertisement. And I am very glad to see you. I am arranging for an interpreter to translate what you have to tell me. Do you understand?"

"Si, señor. I onderstan' ze English, but I spik 'im not well. Pardon!"

"All right. You'll be able to explain things in a few minutes, what!"

As they waited Valdez tried hard to make himself understood.

"Manoel Garcia," he said, "You 'ave took 'im. Ah, no, Señor! 'E 'ave not done so. Manoel Garcia—esmuy bueno caballero—you onderstan'? Yes?"

The Major laid his hand on Valdez' shoulder.

"You shall tell us all about him," he said.

"Si, Señor!"

Major Challow briefly interviewed the bank cashier before taking him into the library.

"You will give me your word, Mr Rothbury," he said, "that you will not divulge to anyone what is about to transpire? Señor Valdez, who is connected with the Coppleswick murder case has just called on me. He speaks very little English, and I want you to be good enough to translate for us. You will understand the importance of secrecy?"

"Perfectly, Major. We bank officials are accustomed to that."

The Chief Constable had also rung up his office in Sydbury, with orders to send his clerk to his private house. This individual arrived just after the cashier, and prepared to take down Ignace Valdez' statement in shorthand.

This statement was, necessarily, slow in its delivery, the interpreter not only having to translate it phrase by phrase, but also to put the questions which the Major interposed from time to time. It is best, therefore, to give an epitome of it.

Señor Valdez commenced by explaining, with a distinct touch of pride, that he was not a Spanish South American, but a true Spaniard, living in Spain. His home was the picturesque little town of Hernani, close to San Sebastian. He was of independent means, in fact he was particularly careful to make the Major understand that he was his social equal, or, perhaps, a little more than his equal.

He had, he went on, a nephew, living in the little State of San Miguel in South America, engaged in engineering work. He had accepted an invitation from this nephew to pay him a long visit, and it was during this visit that he had become acquainted with Felix Nayland. The latter had been on an expedition, following up one of the tributaries of the Amazon through Northern Brazil, and was then resting on his oars in Elizondo, the capital of San Miguel.

Then the insurrection broke out. Neither he nor Nayland nor the nephew wished to take any part in it, though, with an excited populace, it was very difficult for even a foreigner to remain neutral. And, unfortunately, Valdez' nephew happened to be a personal friend of Don Gonzolez, the leader of the insurrection, and, although this nephew had carefully abstained from party politics for this reason, much against his will, he became associated, in the minds of the then dominant party, with the insurrectionists.

Señor Valdez then went on to tell the Chief Constable what he knew about Manoel Garcia. He, himself, was only slightly acquainted with him, having met him once or twice at his nephew's house. Garcia he knew, however, was one of the most honourable citizens of Elizondo, and he and his two sons were ardent supporters of Don Gonzolez. Garcia, when the insurrectionary army was raised, became Aide de Camp to General Zumaya—they seemed to have all been more or less Generals in that army.

Zumaya was one of those characters who generally come to the front in upheavals of Latin races, a mixture of extreme personal bravery, combined with a Machiavellian astuteness. He was the real leader of the whole movement, and under the guise of a military commander, shared, more than anyone else, the knowledge of those secret springs of action which are always at the base of revolutions. A strong man, and a determined man— ruthless when it came to dealing with those who opposed him.

General Zumaya had a wider outlook, also, than most of his compatriots. He had travelled much, and mixed with men of other nationalities. He had, before the insurrection, become very friendly with the young engineer. It may very likely have been for astute purposes of his own, for since he had now risen into power under the presidency of Don Gonzolez, he was said to line his pockets in connection with electric power schemes ostensibly controlled by the government.

Now, for the first time, Señor Valdez mentioned the black ebony box, and Major Challow leaned forward with increased interest. This box, he said, had been presented to his nephew by General Zumaya. It stood on a table in his room, and he used it to keep cigarros in.

"Did he know there was probably a secret division in it?" asked the Major.

Señor Valdez shook his head.

"If he did, he did not tell me," translated the interpreter, "Was there, then, a secret chamber? Yes—Perhaps."

Then he went on to tell the most exciting episode of his story.

His nephew, he said, who lived in a small house in the outskirts of Elizondo, had invited Felix Nayland to dine with them. The three men, having finished their meal, were sitting in the patio over their coffee and cigarros, when they heard shots being fired, and shouting. The next minute General Zumaya and Manoel Garcia came running up, crying out that they had been cut off in a street skirmish, and were being pursued by what *they* called revolutionary troops. All this happened at the juncture when Don Gonzolez had assumed the presidency, the late president had escaped, but order had not yet been restored, and there was still desultory fighting between stray parties of the contending factions.

"What could one do?" said Valdez, throwing out his hands, "one could not see one's friends shot down in cold blood, even if one did not wish to take sides. My nephew at once invited them into his house, and we closed the doors just as the revolutionaries came into view, round the corner of a street. Immediately they opened fire upon us, and shots came through the windows. General Zumaya and Señor Garcia were armed with automatic pistols—and we carried revolvers—it was prudent to do so just then."

"Again," and he threw out his hands once more, "What could one do? We had given them shelter, and we knew now that it was a case of life or death for all five of us. So we returned their fire. My nephew had a packet of cartridges which also fitted Señor Nayland's revolver. He opened it, and divided them. Señor Nayland, who was very calm—he was even smiling, oh, he was a brave man—put his share of the cartridges into the ebony box, which was empty of cigarros, so that he could obtain them the more easily for re-loading."

"It was a big fight. I received a graze in the arm with a bullet, but it was nothing. Only, presently, our stack of cartridge diminished, and it looked very serious, for the enemy approached nearer. We knew they would show us no mercy if they broke into the house. Then Señor Nayland used his last cartridge—he felt for more in the black box, but there were none.

He was angry, and pushed the box away from him, so that it fell on the ground. At that moment a bullet struck General Zumaya in the head, and he fell—close to the box. At first he was not unconscious, he moved, and he spoke a little, but we could not tell what he was saying."

"It was then, just as we imagined that all was over with us, that there was the sound of a volley being fired, and the soldiers of General Zumaya came—not a moment too soon. The other soldiers, they ran away, except some who were captured. So came our relief."

"When we looked around we thought General Zumaya was dead. He lay quite still, and the curious thing was that his hand held the little black box. There was a surgeon among the soldiers who rescued us, he examined Zumaya, and told us he was not yet dead, and there might yet be a chance for him to live."

Señor Valdez then went on to explain that Zumaya was taken to the hospital, where he lay for several weeks in a critical condition, unconscious for the greater part of the time. Ultimately, with the help of skilful surgery and nursing, he recovered.

"But, by that time," added Señor Valdez, "Señor Nayland and I had departed from San Miguel. The Señor Nayland left the day after the fight, in fact, he had come to us for his farewell dinner. And I? I bid adieu to my nephew three weeks afterwards. I intended to go to New York, and afterwards back to Spain, paying a visit to your country—which I had never seen—on my way. And I had promised to pay my respects to Señor Nayland if I did so. He had given me the address of his club in London. Just before I left my nephew was giving me messages to take to my family at Hernani, when, by chance, he looked at the little box on the table. And a thought came into his mind. He said I must take it with me, and give it to Señor Nayland when I met him in England as a memento of the exciting half hour when he had used it for his revolver cartridges. So, in London, I called at this club and was given Señor Nayland's address in the country. I wrote. He invited me to stay with him, and it was then that I presented him with the box. That is all, Señor. And I shall be glad if it will help you—but Manoel Garcia, oh no! He cannot have killed Señor Nayland. Why should he?" and, again, he spread out his hands in expressive gesture.

"I am greatly indebted to you, Señor Valdez," replied the Major, "It is exceedingly good of you to have come to England. And, I need hardly say, that any expenses you have incurred—"

But, as soon as Ignace Valdez understood the purport of these words he drew himself up, indignantly.

"Señor!" he expostulated, "I beg that you will mention no such thing to me. I have only performed what was right."

"I beg your pardon," Major Challow found himself saying, "and now, if I may ask you a question?"

Señor Valdez bowed.

"Did you come across a man named O'Calligan when you were in San Miguel?"

An expression of the deepest contempt spread over the face of the Spaniard.

"I do not know such men," he replied, stiffly, "I have heard of him, yes! He was a despicable traitor. If he journeys to San Miguel again they will shoot him or knife him. And no one will regret it."

"Yes," said Major Challow, "that corresponds with all I know about him. But I want you to tell me something. Do you know if he has any reason for wishing to kill Señor Garcia?"

The Spaniard shrugged his shoulders.

"He would kill anyone who stood in his way," he replied, "He is not a friend of Señor Garcia, it is true—but Señor Garcia has much more reason for killing him—or rather, one of his companions."

"How so?" asked the Major, with extreme interest.

"Pardon!" returned Valdez, "I regret to say words against any compatriot of yours, Señor, for I admire your country. But, in San Miguel there were many bad men—and the worst of them was an Englishman."

"Beech!" growled the Major.

154

"Ah! You have heard? It is true, Señor. And it was Beech who killed, with his own hands, the two sons of Señor Garcia. O'Calligan betrayed them—but it was Beech who murdered them. And, my nephew told me this, Señor Garcia took an oath on the crucifix that he would be revenged—that he would kill Beech when he saw him—and, doubtless, O'Calligan as well."

"What became of Beech?" asked Major Challow, bluntly.

The Spaniard threw out his hands.

"Quien sabe, Señor? It was reported that he was dead, before I left San Miguel. Doubtless there were others who wished for revenge besides Manoel Garcia. Ah, Señor," he went on, "is it permitted for me to speak with Manoel Garcia?"

"Yes," replied the Major, "I will take you to see him at once. But there are certain formalities to be observed. You may say to him, if you please," he went on, "that it would be wise for him to make a statement as to what was in that black box, and why he came to Coppleswick to get it. We shall probably want you again, Señor Valdez. Where are you staying?"

The Spaniard gave him the address of a West End hotel.

"I return there tonight, Señor," he said, "Presently, however, I wish to call on Miss Nayland to pay her my respects, and to condole with her on the loss of her brother—for," and he drew himself up, "the Señor Nayland was my very good friend!"

CHAPTER 14

Señor Valdez duly made his way to Coppleswick to pay his intended call on Miss Nayland. It happened to be the butler's afternoon out, and a maid opened the door to him. She took a little time to understand his broken English at first, apparently, mistaking him for a tout of some kind, but finally showed him into the drawing room where the Vicar, who was calling, was taking tea with Miss Nayland.

Señor Valdez was extremely polite and good mannered, trying very hard to express himself in his limited English. Westerham, who had a very slight knowledge of Spanish, helped him out as well as he could.

Valdez, with great courtesy, condoled with Miss Nayland on the death of her brother.

"He was my good friend," he said, "and it has pained me very much. I offer my sympathy, Señora."

Miss Nayland gave him tea. He explained his presence in England, how he had read of her brother's murder in the Spanish papers, and seen the advertisement that he was wanted. He told them, briefly, the story of the ebony box, and ended up by saying,

"Without doubt the Señor Nayland was the victim of a great mistake. Whoever killed him must have imagined that he was Manoel Garcia,—because he was wearing the coat of Garcia. But it is very strange. Garcia, however, for I have been allowed to see him today, I think will explain who was the man he feared, and will also make plain what was in the box. He has told me that already he has informed the advocate, and the advocate had advised him to say nothing at present."

"I see," said Westerham, "a question of reserving his defence?"

The Spaniard did not understand at first, but Westerham, with some little difficulty, at length explained that when an accused person was before the magistrate, charged with a serious crime, and there was every expectation that he would be committed for trial in any case, the line usually taken by his lawyer was a temporary policy of silence in order that the full defence should be thoroughly worked up for the trial.

Valdez shrugged his shoulders, and threw out his hands.

"Manoel Garcia should not be tried at all," he said, "I am sure he is innocent."

"I think so, too," replied Westerham, "but the law must take its course."

Then Valdez rose to go. Bowing over Miss Nayland's hand he made his polite adieus. And it was then that he expressed a wish to see the scene of the crime.

"If I may?" he said, "But please do not trouble. I remember the garden—when I was here before. I go to look."

"I'll come with you," remarked Westerham, "I have to be getting back, anyway."

And he, too, said goodbye to Miss Nayland.

The two men went out of the house, crossed the lawn, and made their way over the little paddock by the path leading to the pools and the wood. Arrived at the Diana's pool, Westerham explained to the Spaniard what had happened when he and Major Challow had found the body in the water. Valdez, interested and excited, made comments in broken English and Spanish, Westerham following him as well as he could.

"I understand," said Valdez, "It was like this. Manoel Garcia, he came along the path, and Señor Nayland followed him, and spoke to him. Then they went together through the wood—there —and Señor Nayland came back, presently, alone, wearing the green coat. And then, he was murdered, just here—oh, terrible!"

"There is one thing that has always puzzled me," remarked Westerham, half to himself, "What was Nayland doing behind that tree?" and he pointed to the further side of the upper pool.

"Eh? I do not understand," said the Spaniard.

Westerham explained.

"Why," he said, "we found his footprints on the ground behind the tree. It had only been raining for a short time, you know, so they could not have been old impressions. Also there was one of your Spanish cigarette papers—without any gum on it —lying close by. It looks as if he and Garcia had stood there together—though Garcia said, at the inquest, that he did not. It was impossible to tell, because Garcia was wearing rubber soled shoes."

But the Spaniard, who was keenly alert, paid no attention to this detail.

"You found a cigarette paper?" he asked.

"Yes. It could hardly have been Nayland's for he never smoked cigarettes."

"And Manoel Garcia," said Valdez, "he does not smoke at all. He has a malady in the throat. He cannot smoke."

"Is that so?" asked Westerham.

The Spaniard nodded.

"Ah, certainly," he replied, "I know it."

"That's queer," went on Westerham, "Who could it have been?"

"The man who murdered him, perhaps?"

"Yes, but—" said Westerham slowly, "In that case he would have known it was Nayland, and we are supposing that he murdered Nayland thinking he was Garcia; eh?"

The Spaniard threw out his hands.

"It is all very strange," he said, "of one thing I am certain. Manoel Garcia did not kill Señor Nayland, but I know no more. Señor Westerham, excuse me," he added, looking at his watch, "but I return to London. There is a train soon?"

"Yes," said Westerham, also looking at his watch, "at 6.45. More than an hour. Will you come to my house and wait? And allow me to offer you a glass of wine? Then I can run you to the station in my car."

The polite Spaniard raised his hat and bowed.

"You are very kind," he said, "I go with you—with pleasure."

Over his wine Ignace Valdez waxed communicative. Westerham had considerable difficulty in following him at times, for his Spanish was very limited, and the Spaniard talked fast, in the mixture of his own language and as much English as he could command. He got on to the insurrection in San Miguel and the unsought for part he had played in it, and then back to Manoel Garcia.

"You say he lost two sons?" asked Westerham.

"Si, Señor. I did not know them. One was of the age of eighteen and the other twenty. They were both betrayed, O'Calligan was mixed up in it. But the man who actually killed them was this Beech, of whom I have told you—an Englishman who had lived for some years in San Miguel. It was not as if they were slain in a fair fight. They were murdered."

"How did he kill them?" asked Westerham.

"The younger one he shot. He was carrying a message from General Zumaya and Beech, who knew this, had pretended to be his friend. He managed to get him into a house with some others, and asked him for the message, which he would not tell. And Beech drew his revolver and shot him through the heart. With the elder one it was much the same, but he did not shoot him. He threw a knife at him—so!"

And the Spaniard jumped to his feet, and exhibited, in pantomime, the throwing of a knife across Westerham's study. The Vicar shuddered—it was such an essentially foreign action, and Valdez' dark eyes glittered with excitement.

"A bad man," he cried, sitting down once more, "but I think he is dead now. Señor Garcia will never obtain the revenge which he swore. It was even said, in San Miguel, that O'Calligan himself had killed him. For it was known they had quarrelled."

"By the way," said Westerham, for the name had not been mentioned before, "we are speaking in confidence, Señor Valdez? Yes, you mention O'Calligan. Did Manoel Garcia tell you—when you saw him this afternoon—?"

The Spaniard placed a finger on his lips, in significant gesture, and nodded.

"They would not let me see him alone—and they made him talk in English. But, from what he said, I have guessed—and I think his advocate knows. Yes, I believe it was O'Calligan who was here—and—that O'Calligan thought he had killed Garcia."

"Garcia said he was afraid of some man he recognised here."

"He was not afraid!" said Valdez, indignantly, "I think Garcia is a very brave man, yes. What he feared was not O'Calligan himself, but lest O'Calligan should get from him what he found in that box. Oh, yes! Señor Westerham, is it not nearly time for me to go? Excuse! And I thank you, Señor."

Westerham ran him to the station in his car, and then returned to his vicarage. He made his way to his study and sat down at his desk table with the idea of sketching the outlines of a sermon for the following Sunday.

But ideas refused to come. In vain he looked up the Epistle, Gospel and Lessons for that particular Sunday, in the hope of finding a subject from them. His thoughts were continuously straying to those two pools in the wood garden, and the grassy path which lay between them. He was puzzled. After seeing Ignace Valdez he was more than ever convinced that Garcia had not committed the crime. Everything, now, seemed to point towards O'Calligan. Garcia had evidently recognised O'Calligan at the garden party, and the chances were that the recognition had been mutual, for if Nayland had penetrated the disguise of the false beard it was quite probable that O'Calligan had done so, too.

But, what puzzled him chiefly was that if it was O'Calligan, what were he and Nayland doing when the latter was standing behind that tree, if, indeed, O'Calligan had been with him there. That Nayland was there had been pretty conclusively proved.

He pushed Bible and Prayer Book aside, filled and lighted his pipe, and leaned back in his chair, thinking deeply. Presently, with a view to consulting his note book on the case, he pulled open one of the drawers in his writing table. He took out the note book, and, just at that moment, his gaze lighted casually enough, on an open letter lying in the drawer, the letter which Miss Nayland had written to him when she had sent him that parcel of clothes for the jumble sale.

Mechanically his sense of tidiness made him take that letter out of the drawer, intending to tear it up and drop the pieces into the waste-paper basket. As he did so he glanced over the contents.

A sudden exclamation escaped him. He sat there, the letter in his hand, reading it intently. Not a whiff of smoke arose from his pipe, which he still gripped between his teeth—he seemed to have forgotten its presence there, so far as actually smoking it was concerned.

Then he jumped up from his chair and commenced to walk to and fro across his study, still holding Miss Nayland's letter in his hand. Presently he stopped short, and said, out loud in his excitement,

"And Manoel Garcia does not smoke—and—"

A new idea seemed to have seized him. He sat down in his chair again, puffed at his pipe—it was out—relighted it, blew clouds of smoke.

Then he drew the chair up to the table once more, but not for sermon making. Page after page he turned over the leaves of his note book, reading it carefully. And from time to time he jotted something down on a sheet of paper, making so it seemed, a list of something.

In the note book were extracts cut from the local paper containing a verbatim account of the inquest. These he also read, studying the evidence line by line.

He was still engaged in doing this when he heard a car driving up and, looking out of the window, saw that it was Garforth. He swept note book and newspaper extracts back into the drawer, with Miss Nayland's letter, and was, to all intents and purposes, engaged on parochial work when Garforth was shown in.

By this time Westerham had openly become Diana's accepted suitor. Her father was not surprised when the young Vicar interviewed him, for he had marked the growing intimacy. Also, he thoroughly approved of the match, for he liked Westerham immensely, and was glad that his daughter had, chosen him.

"I daresay you can guess why I've dropped in, Harry," he said, using Westerham's Christian name for the first time. "I've just returned from London, and I wanted to see you before I went home. I've had an interview with my son, Harvey, today," he added, tersely.

Westerham nodded sympathetically.

"He's told me everything," went on Garforth, "and you can imagine how I'm feeling. But I'm thankful he made a clean breast of it—and I don't know how to express my obligations to you, Harry."

"Oh, that's nothing, Mr Garforth."

"On the other hand, it's everything. I want to thank you, not only for your tact, but for your solicitude for Diana. You saw, what I can see now I've thought it over, though I couldn't quite grasp it at first—I mean you saw that her sense of honour would have suffered if she had told me, though all the time you knew that I *ought* to be told."

"Well," said Westerham, with the awkwardness of modesty, "I thought that was the best thing to do, you know—and—"

"Indeed it was, and I can't thank you enough."

"I hope," said Westerham, trying to turn the subject from himself, "I hope it's all right about Harvey—I mean that—well— that you haven't dropped on him too heavily."

"It was a painful interview," replied Garforth, a little grimly, "and both of us felt it. But I trust I've done the right thing. I've told him the only way to show his regrets is to stick to his present post and be steady—and that we'll wipe out the past if he can show me a clean sheet at the end of a time of probation I've given him."

"I'm awfully glad of that, sir—and so will Diana be, when you tell her. She's behaved like a heroine over it."

"Yes, she has," replied her father, "and I'm proud of her. I only hope the whole affair, now, will remain a secret between us three."

"And one other—Major Challow," replied Westerham, and explained why he had taken him into his confidence.

"Yes, I see," said Garforth, "I daresay I should have gone to him myself if you hadn't done so. And now, I wonder what is going to happen—if the police get this O'Calligan, I mean."

"I've got some news for you," retorted Westerham, without answering the question. "Who do you think has turned up? Why, Valdez—the fellow who gave Nayland the black box. It's a bit of a story, but I'd like to tell you—if you've time now."

Garforth was only too eager to listen, and the Vicar told him what had happened. When he had finished, the barrister said,

"Well, all I can say is, the case is becoming more and more complicated. First, there's Garcia. The police wouldn't have asked for a second remand if they'd been certain of their evidence against him. It shows they have doubts, and this fellow Valdez must have increased those doubts. I said the other day I wouldn't mind taking up the defence professionally if it came to a trial, but I have my suspicion that it won't now. And, anyhow, under the new circumstances, I couldn't touch it—for they concern my own family."

"And as to O'Calligan," he went on, "it looks ugly there. If the police get him—and I suppose they're after him—they'll have two men to charge with the crime—unless they withdraw the charge against Garcia. It's precious awkward for them. I should think Challow must be a bit worried over it. I wonder what line he'll take."

Westerham was looking hard at the other. When the latter had finished, he said,

"You think O'Calligan did it?"

Garforth shrugged his shoulders.

"It looks very much like it," he said, "Personally, I wish he was out of it. It means Diana will have to give evidence. You think he did it, don't you, Harry?"

Westerham was some moments before he answered. Then he said, slowly,

"I—don't—know! I've got hold of a queer notion."

163

"What is it?"

But the Vicar shook his head.

"I won't say, yet," he replied, "very likely I'm a bit of a fool and have been letting my imagination run away with me. But I'm going to put my theory to the test, if I can, all the same. Afterwards, I'll tell you—whether it's right or wrong. By the way, do you happen to know the name of the boat that Nayland came back in from South America?"

"Yes—I do. The 'Pelican'."

"What line?"

"'Blue Diamond'. But why?"

Westerham laughed.

"No," he said, "I'm not going to let anything out."

Then Garforth got up to go.

"Shall we see you at 'Beechcroft' this evening? Won't you run home with me and dine? Or come in afterwards."

But Westerham shook his head.

"Tell Di I'm awfully sorry," he replied, "But I've got a lot to do tonight."

"Come and lunch tomorrow then. It's an off day with me."

"And tomorrow I have to run up to London, but I'll get around in the evening if I can."

And when Garforth had departed the Vicar got out his note book again, and studied it until the bell rang for the evening meal. And, after the meal, he went out, crossed the lane at the back of his house, and made his way, through the wood, to the spot where Nayland had been murdered. For quite a long time he remained there, viewing it from several points. And the point which seemed to attract him most was that spot, behind the tree, where Detective Sergeant Ringwood had found the imprints of Felix Nayland's boots, and both he and Westerham had observed that tiny scrap of tissue paper with the edges ungummed.

CHAPTER 15

Major Challow sat in the Chief Constable's office at the Sydbury Police Station, stern of feature, and monocle in his eye. Beside the door, as if to guard it, stood the Superintendent and Detective Sergeant Ringwood, the latter in plain clothes. And, in front of the Major, in easy, almost nonchalant attitude, was a man of between thirty and forty years of age, faultlessly dressed, with close cropped red hair and small, toothbrush moustache of the same aggressive colour, bright, rather impudent eyes, and refined features. And, as he faced the Chief Constable, a little, sarcastic smile curved his lips.

"Your name is Patrick Maria O'Calligan?" asked the Major.

"Quite correct," replied the other.

"Your domicile?"

O'Calligan shrugged his shoulders, and laughed.

"Wherever I happen to be, sir. I may, perhaps, describe myself as an international."

The Major took no notice of this impertinent answer.

"You understand," he said, with that dignified sternness which he could so well assume, "that you are charged with a very serious crime, that of being accessory to the murder of Felix Nayland."

"So this—er—gentleman," pointing to Detective Sergeant Ringwood, "has already informed me."

"And that anything you say will be taken down and may be used as evidence?" went on Major Challow.

"Perfectly. But I have a good deal to say, sir, and I don't mind in the least if it is used as evidence. I shall use it myself as evidence, or my counsel will—if I have to submit to the farce of a trial."

"I've warned you," replied the Major, severely. "You can make a statement if you wish to—but you need not. Also, you are at liberty to consult a solicitor."

"I see," replied O'Calligan. "Well, I would like to make a statement to begin with. And, by the way, may I ask what Manoel Garcia—who, I understand, you are keeping as another potential murderer, has to say about me?"

"That I cannot tell you," replied the Major, "nor is it in order for you to put such questions."

"I see! Your British idea of justice, eh? Well, let's get to work. Who is going to do the scribbling?"

Indignantly the Major nodded to the Superintendent, who took his place at the table.

"Shorthand?" asked the prisoner, cheerfully, "or shall I speak slowly? And I hope you're a good speller."

"I shall take it down in shorthand," replied the Superintendent, curtly.

"Good. Not such a lengthy process. Well, to begin with, it must be evident to *you*, sir," and he turned to Major Challow, "that it is no use for me to deny that I was at Mr Nayland's garden party. *You* saw me there. And I saw you. I thought, of course, you were an ordinary gentleman then. I didn't know you were a policeman."

The Major grunted indignantly, but said nothing.

"I *was* there. Though I was not invited. I'll try to be brief. Coming over recently from South America I made, on the boat, the acquaintance of rather a young ass named Harvey Garforth. I call him an ass, because his ideas of poker were abominable—and unfortunate for him. He lost. I won. Like the man in the parable, he had not sufficient to pay—in cash, so he gave me a certain stamped document. Shall I tell you what it was?"

"No," replied the Major, "there is no necessity for that."

"Exactly. I gather you probably know already. If so, you will agree that if one can avoid scandal, it is best. Well, this particular document, so it appeared to me, had a certain value above that which it bore on its face. I imagined that his family might be prepared to purchase it—at a price. Please don't call the transaction by the ugly term of blackmail—we will look upon it as a business proposition. For certain reasons I though Garforth's sister would more readily pay the price than her father—women are always more impulsive, so I motored down from London to see her. The maid at her house told me she had gone to a garden party close by. I made a few inquiries, and, finding it was a large affair, thought I could saunter in unobserved—for I did not wish my journey to be in vain.

"I parked my car—and I want you to observe this—with a lot of others, in a field partly behind the house, a field that bordered the road at the back of it, and made my way on to the lawn. I very soon discovered who was Miss Garforth, spoke to her, and arranged a private interview in the wood. This took place, when, I believe, some sort of a concert was going on in the hall of the house. I explained to Miss Garforth why I had come, and, in a short time, we arrived at a mutual understanding—she was willing to accept my terms and redeem this—er—document. So we parted. She went on through the wood, and I was about to return to the house when—I have a stray sense of locality—it occurred to me I could get to my car by striking across the wood, and so avoid any further risk—for I had noticed several people eyeing me curiously."

"This I did, and soon came out to the field where the cars were parked. It struck six by some clock in the neighbourhood just as I did so. The cars were beginning to leave the field. I remember speaking to one of the chauffeurs, and I also remember the registration number of his car—PZ 7777—the sequence of 'seven,' I suppose, impressed me. You will find he will corroborate this, I expect."

Major Challow and Ringwood both made notes, "Mrs Leigh-Hulcott's car," remarked the former; and the Major nodded.

"That is all," went on O'Calligan, "I have explained why I came to Coppleswick. You may ask Miss Garforth, and, if she speaks the truth, she will tell you the same. As for committing a murder," and he shrugged his shoulders, "nothing of the kind. I did not know Nayland. I had every reason for avoiding him there. And as to being in collusion with Manoel Garcia—well—" and he shrugged his shoulders, "I did not notice him under his disguise there, though, from what I read about the inquest, he appears to think I did. If I had—well, I had certain reasons for avoiding him as well as Mr Nayland."

He paused. The Major made no comment. He only asked if this was all that O'Calligan had to say.

The other bowed.

"It will be written out," went on the Major, "and you will be called upon to sign it. There is another formality to be gone through now, Superintendent?"

The latter nodded, got up, unlocked a cupboard and took from it two or three tin slabs, and some printer's ink. O'Calligan watched him with interest.

"You're going to take my finger prints?" he asked the Major.

"Yes," said the latter, curtly.

"Good! I should have suggested it myself if you hadn't. A most excellent idea—when one has a clear conscience and is innocent!"

The Superintendent carefully spread a thin film of printer's ink over one of the tin slabs. Then he placed a sheet of white paper on the table. He took what is known as a "rolled" impression of the thumbs and fingers of the prisoner. He made O'Calligan place each finger on the inked slab, the plane of the nail being at right angles to the plane of the slab, and then turn the finger over till the bulb surface, which first of all faced to the left, now faced to the right, the plane of the nail being again at right angles to the slab.

Each finger, thus inked, was then "rolled" in a similar manner, only very lightly, on the surface of the white paper, leaving a complete impression. The paper, thus inked, was carefully set aside to be photographed, and, with a curt nod of dismissal on the part of the Major, O'Calligan, smiling and debonair, was taken out of the room by Ringwood, to be consigned to a cell.

Then the Major looked at the Superintendent.

"Well?" he asked, abruptly.

"I don't like it, sir. That's a fact. You probably know more than I do about this affair of Miss Garforth?" Major Challow nodded, "what do you think of it sir?"

"He was in the wood at the time of the murder, by his own admission," said the Chief Constable.

"Or just *before!*" retorted the Superintendent, drily, "we don't know the exact moment of the murder—and there's a distinct difficulty?

"In spite of his glibness—it looks suspicious," went on the Chief Constable, "especially if he mistook Nayland for Garcia. The finger prints may help us."

"Don't you count on *that*, sir," replied the Superintendent, "I'll have them taken up to Scotland Yard tomorrow—for expert opinion. But—well, I'm afraid there won't be much in it. Yes? Come in!" for there was a tap at the door.

Keston, the lawyer came into the office.

"Oh," he said, "I thought I might find you here, Major Challow —no—don't go, Superintendent," he went on, as the latter moved towards the door, "you might as well hear what I have to say, too. It's about my client, Garcia. I've just been seeing him."

"Yes?" asked the Major.

"It's a little out of order, perhaps. But he wants to make a further statement. I have cautioned him about the matter, but the visit of this Spaniard—Valdez, isn't that his name—seems to have influenced him. He had already told me a good deal—in order that I might prepare his defence—but he says, now, that there is no reason why he should keep back anything from the authorities, and he would prefer you to know all the facts. On careful consideration I see no objection to his action. After all, these facts are only supplementary to those which you already know—which he told at the inquest."

"We don't ask for a further statement; you know that?" replied the Major.

"Of course. You would be out of order in doing so, with

the charge against him. But, perhaps I may suggest that, as I understand another arrest has been made, you may have difficulties in pressing that charge?"

But Major Challow was too wary to be caught like that.

"What would that have to do with it?" he asked.

"Oh, I was merely suggesting that further information might assist you. I know," and he laughed lightly, "that it is not for the defence to help the prosecution—only—you see in this particular instance the accused definitely wishes that you should receive a further statement from him. And I can't stop him."

"Oh," said the Major, with a laugh, "that's it, is it? What! I think I see. You might like to have our opinion on this statement, eh, Mr Keston? Well, you won't, you know. What!"

The lawyer only laughed in return.

"All right, Major," he said, "I should certainly have liked to hear your comments, but I quite understand. Anyhow, I may say, without prejudice, you know, that I am, personally, convinced of my client's innocence. And *you* don't want to hang the wrong man, I fancy—goodbye!"

He laughed again as he went out. He and the Major were very good friends in private life, and he could afford a little chaff.

"Isn't that like a lawyer, what?" said Major Challow, as soon as he had gone out, "evidently tried to prevent Garcia from making this statement; then, when he found the man was bent upon doing it in spite of him, tries to get out of us what *we* think! Well, I'll go and see the fellow at once. You'll be wanting to get on with those finger prints. Better send one of your men up to Scotland Yard with them at once, and tell him to bring back a report."

"Very good, sir."

When the Major entered Garcia's cell, together with a shorthand clerk, he greeted his prisoner, not, indeed, with affability, but, at the same time, with official courtesy. Garcia returned the greeting, rising to do so.

"You have everything you want, I hope?" asked the Major.

"Except my liberty," replied Garcia, "Yes, sir—I have no

complaints to make about my treatment."

"Your solicitor has told me you wish to make a further statement?"

"That is true."

The Chief Constable cautioned him, ending up by saying,

"I want you thoroughly to understand that our English Law, which I represent, does not require you to do or say anything that may prejudice your defence."

"Thank you. Yes. I understand. But I wish to tell you. It is what I would not tell at the inquest—an explanation. Señor Valdez, however, has already made plain to you the part I played under Don Gonzolez?"

Major Challow nodded.

"What I wish to avoid," went on Garcia, "if it is possible, is that what I am about to tell you should be made public."

"Then you will be wise not to tell me," retorted the Major, "I have already warned you that it may be used in evidence."

"I know that. And it will be used as evidence in my defence if I am sent to a judge to be tried. I must then use it myself, through my advocate. But I have thought that if I tell you now it may help you to deal with my case. For," and he smiled as he looked at the Chief Constable, "it has come into my mind, sir, that you are not so positive as you were that I killed Señor Nayland. You make much delay."

The Major's smile, returning that of his prisoner, was a grim one.

"Our methods are sometimes slow," he retorted. "You must not count on *that*."

Garcia shrugged his shoulders, and began.

"Señor Ignace Valdez had told you of the fight in his nephew's house at Elizonda? When my chief, General Zumaya was badly wounded?" he asked.

"Yes."

"Then you will the better understand what I have to tell you. Señor Valdez does not know the real reason why my chief and I were attacked that day. It was because General Zumaya had in his possession a very important document—only half a sheet of note paper, but what was written upon it involved the lives of a dozen or more men. It was a list of citizens of San Miguel who had been playing what perhaps you call in your language a "shady game." Is that not your slang expression? Yes? They were, outwardly, partizans of the late government, but, secretly, were on the side of Don Gonzolez. You will understand, sir, that in an insurrection there are those whose patriotism does not come first with them, and yet, all the time, it is necessary to make use of them?"

The Major's reply was a single word.

"Machiavellian!" he murmured.

"Yes—I understand. And it is true. Now those who pursued us that day knew that General Zumaya carried this list—they had their spies. And if they had captured it everyone on that list would have died very suddenly—sooner or later. Even if Don Gonzolez triumphed—as he has done—it would have been the same. When the General was struck by the bullet and fell he remained conscious only for a minute or two—and he thought it was the end—that the enemy was about to break into the house. For himself, he cared not—he is a brave man; but he remembered that little piece of paper. And a sudden idea struck him. Lying on the ground before him was that ebony box which he himself had presented to Señor Valdez' nephew. But only General Zumaya knew that there was a secret connected with it, for he had never thought to tell that secret to Valdez' nephew. By pressing a certain part of it one of the inner sides fell away, and there was a tiny cavity behind."

"In the noise and excitement not one of us saw the General open this little secret place, take the folded paper from his tunic, and put it inside the cavity. Almost as soon as he had done so he became unconscious, and it was three weeks later before, in the hospital, his senses returned."

"Then he remembered. He sent for me and told me. He ordered me to get that box from the young man and bring it to him. But, by that time, Señor Valdez had taken the box away, as you know,

172

and had departed to New York. I found out, without arousing the suspicion of Valdez' nephew, that he had sent it to Señor Nayland, but that it might be many weeks before he delivered it. All this I told General Zumaya."

"And Zumaya said that the list of names must be recovered. It was the only authentic one. There was no copy. It had been compiled with much trouble and danger by one of our spies who had, himself, been stabbed to death just after he had despatched it to the General. And General Zumaya had not even had time to read it when we were ambushed. *No one* knew what was on it."

"So I had my orders. I was to come to England, I and another compatriot—but not together. His name was De Soto. He came by one route, I by another. I had his address in London, and it was agreed that I should take him the box when I had obtained it. You wonder why, sir? It is very simple. De Soto was an unknown man. I was well known. De Soto was to carry the box back to General Zumaya. I was to remain in England for a few weeks afterwards to allay suspicion. Again you wonder why? It was because we know O'Calligan was here. And O'Calligan was a *very* clever man. If he saw me in England he might guess why I had come. But he would not know De Soto."

"There is not much more to say. You know how I pretended to be one of the Band in order to get into Señor Nayland's house. It was foolish, I can see. I ought to have taken Señor Nayland into my confidence, but most of us are fools at times, especially those times when we try to be very clever. I was prepared to search the house—I had thought no one would be inside, because of the party, but almost the first thing I saw when I entered the hall was the box."

"You know the rest. Señor Nayland followed me, and I had to explain. To prove that I spoke the truth I broke the box—I did not understand the secret opening. And there was the paper. The Señor Nayland at once helped me to escape—I had told him I had seen O'Calligan on the lawn, and, of course, I thought O'Calligan had followed me there."

"As soon as I reached London that night I sought De Soto, and gave him the paper—having first put it into a sealed envelope. He was going back to Rio by the next boat. But, at the inquest, I knew the boat had not yet started, and I dared not speak the truth. That was why I was silent. Now," and he threw out his hands, "it is different. By this time I think General Zumaya has the paper—and it is all finished. That is what I wished to tell you, sir, and perhaps you may think it advisable to communicate privately with General Zumaya. But that is in your hands."

Major Challow made no comments. But his mind strayed to the Foreign Office and code cablegrams; and he wondered if there was an English Consul in San Miguel.

"When your statement is written out, you will sign it, please," he said.

"Assuredly."

When the Major regained his office, he sent at once for the Superintendent.

"Have you sent a man up to Scotland Yard, yet?" he asked brusquely—"about those finger prints."

"Not yet, sir. We shall have a photograph in half an hour's time."

"Very well, I'll take 'em myself, what! I'll go home and pack a bag, as I shall stay the night in London. Send the photos to my house, as soon as they're ready, please. You can get Garcia's signature to his statement when it's written out. Read it. They're a hectic lot of johnnies over in San Miguel, you'll find, what!"

*

"Out of the question, sir," said the Scotland Yard expert, when he had laboriously examined the prints of O'Calligan's thumb and fingers, and compared them with the faint, broken impression which had been found on the handle of the knife which killed Felix Nayland, "Couldn't possibly be the same. They're two absolutely distinct types, you see. The one on the knife handle, faint as it is, is what we call a 'Whorl' type, with a double cone, and bifurcated ridges. This," and he pointed to O'Calligan's, "is a

174

'Composite', with combinations of the Arch and Loop."

"I see," replied Major Challow, "Well, I'm not altogether surprised. But it doesn't make the case any more simple, confound it, what!"

It was too late to call at the Foreign Office that day, but Major Challow went there the next morning and again interviewed the Assistant Secretary.

"It's a rum story, Major," he said, when he'd heard it, "got the true Spanish American colour about it, though. I daresay it's true. Yes, we'll cable our man out there—cipher, of course. Ask him to see this firebrand, Zumaya. Can't be certain that he'll corroborate it, of course. But we'll do our best."

Major Challow, as he travelled back to Sydbury that day, in rather a testy humour, read his newspaper. There was a headline —not on the front page now, for other matters had claimed that position—"The Coppleswick Murder." "Another arrest," and a brief paragraph, not giving O'Calligan's name, but stating that it was understood that the police had detained a man on suspicion. He turned over the leaf—a short "leader" on the Coppleswick Case, accusing the provincial police of lethargy and stupidity. And the Major, remembering the work of the last twenty-four hours, dashed the paper on the floor of the compartment, and, very heartily, ejaculated, "Damn!"

CHAPTER 16

The Vicar of Coppleswick had come back from his visit to London. This visit had been very brief, for he was home again by the early afternoon and had completed a round of parochial visits before he sat down to his tea.

Westerham always enjoyed his tea, and made no secret of it. He often said that his brain power was never better than after three cups of strong tea, and it was immediately after this meal, if he was able to manage it, that he generally worked out his sermons, or tackled difficult correspondence, or those parochial problems of the desk and study about which few of the laity know very much.

But, on this particular occasion, the parish correspondence, and his sermons were set on one side. First of all he devoted himself to the note book in which he had made so many careful entries concerning the death of Felix Nayland. And he jotted down one or two more sentences on that slip of paper on which he had made extracts the previous evening. Then he looked at the clock on his mantlepiece. The hands pointed at a few minutes after six. He smiled grimly to himself as he remembered that this was the hour which was associated with the murder.

At half past seven he would be having his simple evening meal. At eight there was a confirmation class—that would be over in half an hour, for he did not believe in prolonging instruction to the young. At nine he wanted to run over to "Beechcroft" and see Diana—he had not been able to get there for a couple of days.

But, before any of these things happened, he had a problem to solve. He wanted to get five minutes with James Burt, the butler at "The Pleasaunce." He had one or two questions he wished to ask him. But he particularly wanted to see him in a casual sort of manner, as if by accident. How was he to do this?

He visualised the establishment at "The Pleasaunce." Outside, there was the gardener, who also acted as chauffeur, and a boy who helped him—that boy, by the way, was coming to his confirmation class presently. They both left off work at six o'clock—and went home. Inside, there were Burt, the butler, the cook, and a house parlour maid. So far as his recollection served him today was the latter's afternoon and evening out. So much the better. And he formed his plan accordingly. Taking a sheet of writing paper he penned the following,

DEAR MISS NAYLAND:
I think your brother had among the books in his library Fraser's "Golden Bough." It is a work of several volumes. Might I be allowed to borrow it. I rather want it this evening, if it won't trouble you too much to send it to me.
With kind regards,
Yours very sincerely,
H. WESTERHAM.

He smiled as he read this letter over. Then he put it into an envelope, directed the latter to Miss Nayland, and rang the bell.

"Oh," he said, as a maid came in, "I want you to take this note to Miss Nayland at once. There's no answer, so as soon as you have left it you needn't wait."

"Very well, sir."

When she had gone he opened the French window of his study. This window commanded the approach to the Vicarage; anyone coming either to front or back door was bound to pass within view of it. He waited, till he saw the maid returning, and called to her through the window,

"You left my note, Alice?"

"Yes, sir."

"You didn't wait for an answer?"

"No, sir. You told me not to."

"Quite right!"

Then he waited again, quietly smoking his pipe, and a quick gleam shone for a moment in his eye when, after a bit, he saw Burt, in his black suit, wearing a bowler hat, coming up the path, carrying a brown paper parcel under his arm. His little ruse had succeeded.

"Oh, Burt!" he called, but without getting up from the chair in which he was seated a little way back from the window, "are those the books I asked your mistress to lend me? You might bring them here."

The butler turned aside from the carriage drive, crossed the lawn, and came up to the window.

"Come in," invited the Vicar, and Burt entered the room through the French window, taking off his hat respectfully as he did so.

"Miss Nayland's compliments, sir," he said, "and she hopes these are the volumes you require."

"Oh, thank you," replied Westerham, "I'll have a look. Take a seat, Burt, won't you?"

"Thank you, sir," said Burt, and sat down on the edge of a chair, bolt upright, in that deferential attitude which a well trained servant adopts when he is asked to sit down in the presence of his superiors.

Westerham leisurely cut the string and unwrapped the parcel, making casual remarks about the weather as he did so.

"Yes," he said, presently, "these are the books I wanted. Thank you for bringing them, Burt."

The butler was in the act of rising from his chair, but Westerham, who was an easy and natural talker, made several further remarks. At length, in quite an ordinary way, he introduced the subject of the murder.

"Well," he said, "you haven't been called upon to give evidence against Garcia yet, I see."

"No, sir. Though it's very little I have to say."

"He comes up again on Saturday," remarked Westerham, "I'm a witness, of course, but they haven't called me yet. Shockingly slow these police are! I can't make out why they delay so much."

"They are slow, sir. Do you suppose we shall be wanted on Saturday?"

"Ah, that's just what I want to know myself," said the Vicar, "if not, I want to play golf. Might as well see. Wait a minute, Burt—I'll ring up the police at Sydbury. Then we shall both know—and if we're wanted, I'll run you there in my car."

"That's very kind of you, sir."

Westerham's telephone was in his study. He rang up the police station and waited. When he was through, he began,

"Hullo! Mr Westerham of Coppleswick Vicarage speaking—yes—are you Superintendent Fraser? All right—tell him I want him for a moment—thanks—Yes? You're the Superintendent? Right! Well, look here, I wonder if you can tell me whether I shall be wanted on Saturday to give evidence—yes—yes—Garcia—that's what I mean—And Burt—Nayland's butler, you know, would be glad to know, too—he's here with me now—quite so—oh!—yes, yes. I see. Then you'll let me know—yes—thanks. Good night, Superintendent."

He turned to Burt.

"He's not quite sure yet, he says. There may be a further remand, and, in that case, we shan't be wanted. But he'll let us know. Let me see, today's Wednesday. There's plenty of time. By the way, Burt, you've never actually seen this fellow Garcia, since you observed him crossing the lawn—with your master following, have you? You weren't at the adjourned inquest, if I remember rightly?"

"No, sir. I haven't seen him since then. I didn't have to give evidence at the adjourned inquest."

"Oh, yes. Of course. I see," he went on, casually, "that the police have made another arrest—or detained someone."

"So I observed in yesterday's paper, sir. Have—you any idea who he is, sir?"

"Can't say," replied Westerham, "perhaps he's someone who knows Garcia. Anyhow, I shouldn't think there's much doubt about Garcia himself. Oh, well—you'll give my compliments to Miss Nayland, Burt, and thank her for these books."

"Very good, sir."

"Oh, by the way," went on Westerham as Burt once again rose to go, "I wonder if you can help me—you're a butler, and it ought to be in your line. Are you a judge of wine, Burt?"

"To a certain extent, sir. Mr Nayland sometimes consulted me when he was about to purchase any."

"Good! Well, I'd like your opinion. I don't know much about the subject myself, but I like to have something for my friends, and the other day I bought two dozen of Chateau Yquan at a sale. At least, that's how it was listed, but I've got an idea it's something inferior—Petits Cotes, you know, is sometimes passed off as Chateau Yquan. I wish you'd tell me."

"If I can, sir."

"All right. Sit down again, then, and I'll fetch a bottle."

Westerham went out of the room, returning presently with a bottle of wine, a small claret tumbler on a tray, and a corkscrew. He drew the cork and poured out a glass of wine.

"Try it," he said, "and tell me what you think of it."

The butler sipped it in approved manner, smelt it, and finally drained the glass.

"Well?" asked Westerham.

"It's Chateau Yquan, I think, sir," replied Burt, "but, as you say, it seems a little inferior. Not enough body in it, I should say."

"Exactly. Just what I thought. Have another glass, Burt."

"Thank you, sir."

He drank the second glass and took his leave. Westerham slowly filling his pipe, stood by the French window, watching him. Then, glancing at his clock, which now marked a quarter to seven, he wrote a letter, sealed it, and locked it up in his desk. When he went out of the room he took away the opened wine bottle, tray and glass.

The bell rang for his meal at seven, but Westerham, who was

a very punctual man, did not take his seat at the table till ten minutes past. He hurried through the meal. At half past seven he was back in his study, welcoming half-a-dozen village lads, who came in a body, rather shy and reserved, according to their kind.

He wondered as he tried to instil into them the simple elements of the Christian Faith that evening, whether they were really taking it in. They sat in a semicircle around him, perfectly well behaved, but, for the most part, silent and, apparently, unresponsive. Now and again he drew an answer from one or two of them, when he lapsed into the catechetical method of instruction. But it was difficult to tell if they were at all impressed.

Just before he finished he was enlarging upon truthfulness. He knew perfectly well, from experience, how lightly the truth is often regarded by those who have only received what is at best a smattering of education, how easy it is for them, if not exactly to tell a direct lie, at all events to evade or keep back the truth when it might lead to a little trouble or something a bit disagreeable. It was this particular point that he was discussing. Presently he closed the class, said good night to the lads, and stood, holding the door open, while they passed out.

All but one, a tall, gawky looking fellow, with an honest, but not particularly intelligent face, by name George Allen, who worked under the gardener at "The Pleasaunce." He lingered, awkwardly, shifting from foot to foot, and twisting his cap in his hands. And Westerham guessed, by his manner, that he had something to say—if he could get it out.

"Yes?" he said, "you want to speak to me, George?"

"Yes, sir."

"All right, sit down again, then. What is it? You want to ask me about anything I've been telling you?"

There was a little pause. Then George Allen made an effort.

"It's like this, sir. You said just now that if a chap makes out as he's speaking the truth, when he ain't said all of it, he's a liar."

"Well, in a way he is, George. Suppose the keeping back of something means injury to another person—it's very much the same as if he told that other person a direct lie, isn't it, now?"

George thought a moment, and then said,

"I ain't no wish to be a liar, sir—'specially just now, wi' this confirmation job acomin' on."

It was crudely put, but the Vicar was delighted. It meant that his instructions had been responded to after all.

"If you've told lies, George," he said, "you must ask God to forgive you. And, as I've told you all, you can make your confession to me or to some other clergyman, if you want to."

George Allen's reply was startling, but thoroughly characteristic. Fortunately Westerham had too keen an insight into the psychology of the village youth to imagine that the lad meant to insult him, when he said,

"I ain't no liar, sir, and it's nought to do with you nor with another parson. T'aint your business."

"All right, then. I don't ask you to tell me any more—whatever it is."

"Only," went on George, stolidly, and ignoring the other, "What you said tonight set me thinkin' and I see what you mean. I hadn't thought a chap might do harm by holding his tongue when he wasn't asked to say nought."

"Well, it may be like that, George."

"Ah! I knows what to do now—but it ain't no concern o' yours, sir, straight it ain't. Good night, sir!"

Westerham smiled to himself as the lad went out of the room. Evidently he had something on his conscience, and wanted to put it right. And that was all to the good. The evening had not been wasted.

But the evening was not over yet—a quarter past eight. At last he was free to run round to Diana. There was one thing to be done first, though. And, again, he rang up the police station at Sydbury.

"Hullo—yes—Mr Westerham speaking—is Detective Sergeant Ringwood about—I want a word with him—yes—very well."

For the reply came through that the Sergeant was on the premises, but in another office. Would Westerham hold the line while they sent for him.

In a few moments he heard Ringwood's voice speaking, and the following conversation took place,

"I want to see you, Ringwood."

"Yes, sir. I shall be free tomorrow morning."

"That won't do. I must see you tonight."

"Is it important, sir? I'm very busy."

"Yes—it is important. If necessary I'll motor in—presently."

"Don't trouble to do that, Mr Westerham. I've got a motor bike. If it's urgent I'll run out tonight."

"It is rather urgent. What time will you come?"

There was a short pause, and then,

"I can't get away till ten, Mr Westerham, but it will only take me twenty minutes to run out. Will that be too late for you?"

"Not at all. Suit me very well. I've got an engagement lasting till ten. I'll look out for you at about twenty past."

He heaved a sigh of relief, hurried to his garage, and in five minutes time was running at high speed to "Beechcroft." He had, at first, to be polite to his future father-in-law, but in a very short time he was seated in a remote summer house, his arm around Diana's waist. And the conversation did *not* turn on the Coppleswick murder case. The conversation was quite apart from this story—but the gist of it is being eternally repeated whenever a man and a maid meet together under the auspices of the little blind God.

As, later on, he was saying good night to Garforth, the latter remarked,

"I see the police have made another arrest—O'Calligan, I suppose. So there are likely to be further developments. Well, it looks as if Di will have to face the music in the witness box. It can't be helped."

"I think there may be further developments," replied Westerham, enigmatically, "but I'm rather hoping that Di's evidence won't come off. Good night!"

"Eh—what?"

But Westerham had gone, swiftly, out of the room, and

Garforth was too much of a sportsman to interfere with the more lingering good nights that were being said at the hall door.

Soon after ten Westerham was seated in his study once more. The servants had gone to bed. He was smoking comfortably, leaning back in one chair, his feet up in another, resting with the air of a man who has done his work for the day, and is satisfied with it. As he heard the "chug-chug" of a motor bike coming towards the house, he made his way to the front door, and was standing on the step outside when Ringwood drove up.

"Awfully good of you to come, Sergeant," he said, as the detective got off his bicycle.

"Oh, that's all right, Mr Westerham—especially if you've got any information for me."

"Come inside," retorted Westerham, and led the way to the study.

"You'd like a drink after your ride, Sergeant?"

"Thank you, Mr Westerham. I won't refuse."

"Sorry I haven't any whisky in the house. But I'll get you something else. Sit down, won't you?"

He returned in a minute or two with a tumbler and the bottle out of which Burt had poured himself two glasses of Chateau Yquan.

"Try this," he said—"All right, eh?"

"By George, that's good stuff, sir!"

Westerham laughed.

"You're not such a connoisseur as Burt, Miss Nayland's butler," he said, "he didn't think much of it. All the same, I hope it's going to help to settle a little problem."

"What's that?" asked the detective, a puzzled look breaking over his face.

"All in good time. Now, look here, Ringwood, I haven't asked you to come out for nothing. But you must let me do things in my own way. It's a fancy I have. You want to get to the bottom of this Coppleswick case, don't you?"

"Good Lord, yes. Of course I do, sir. What—?"

But Westerham held up his hand.

184

"No! Let me go on. You've got Garcia and you've got O'Calligan
—"

"How—"

"Don't interrupt, please! Now, we're speaking in confidence, and anything you say won't be taken down and used as evidence. This is strictly between ourselves, my friend. Honestly, which of the two do *you* think murdered Felix Nayland?"

The detective looked at Westerham in silence for a few moments. Then he said,

"There you get me, Mr Westerham. Honestly—between ourselves—I don't know what to think. I've never handled such a queer case."

"You've handled it very well, Sergeant—excellently. You couldn't have done more. Now there's another question I want to ask you. I asked you before, but you wouldn't answer me—you were quite right, too. But I want you to be frank with me now, and I believe—I don't say I'm certain—mind you, but I believe it's going to pay you to be frank with me. Did you find any finger prints on the handle of the knife that killed Nayland?"

The detective hesitated for a moment. But quickly made up his mind,

"Yes—we did. A very faint and broken thumb print—but not too faint or broken to be identified."

"Very well. Another question. Mind, I wouldn't ask it without a good reason, and that reason is not my own curiosity. I presume you have taken Garcia's and O'Calligan's finger prints. Well, did either of them correspond with the one on the knife handle?"

"Hang it all—*no*; they didn't. And there's the weak point, sir."

"Exactly. Now, I'm not a detective, Ringwood, but you were good enough once to give me credit for observation. Well, I am observant. And, not only that, but I'm a bit fond of finding out where my observations lead me to. You have your professional note book, in which you enter up all you think relates to a crime. I've got my amateur one—it's in there," and he pointed to the drawer in his writing case, "and I've entered up every detail

I've observed concerning my friend's death. Out of your notes, I presume you formulate a theory. Well, it's taken a long time, but I've formulated *my* theory. I've got it sketched out, along with the note book. It may or it may not be true, but it accounts, in every detail, not only for the manner in which Nayland was murdered, but for the motive."

"May I see it, Mr Westerham?" asked Ringwood, eagerly.

"Not tonight," replied Westerham, "no—you mustn't be disappointed. You shall see it, but there's something I want you to do first. Now, look here. You want to bring this case to a successful conclusion, don't you?"

"Why, naturally, Mr Westerham. Of course I'm on my mettle, so to speak, and I'd like to pull it off."

"All right. Whatever I may have discovered you shall have the credit of. That's only fair. I might have gone to Major Challow about it, I know. But I haven't. You and I, in a way, joined hands when we were the first to notice that ungummed cigarette paper —and I think I know its bearing on the case now. We're in partnership, Ringwood, but I'm only a sleeping partner. See?"

"It's very generous of you, Mr Westerham, I'm sure."

"Don't say that till you're certain that my theory has anything in it. Now, then, will you trust me, Ringwood?"

"Certainly I will sir."

"Very well. Wait a minute."

He unlocked a drawer in his writing table, opened it, and drew out the letter he had written before dinner that evening, together with a small square package, looking like a box, wrapped in brown paper, tied up and sealed.

"Perhaps," he said, with a little laugh, "I'm a bit melodramatic. Anyhow it's my way of going to work. Now, Sergeant Ringwood, I want you to put this little parcel in your pocket—be careful with it, please—and the letter. Then go straight home, and, when you get there, *open the letter first*—before you tackle the parcel. Do you understand?"

"I understand what you say, sir, but I can't catch your meaning."

"You will—when you read that letter. You said you'd trust me. Act upon what's written there. I warn you it may come to nothing, but I also tell you it's worth trying."

"I'll do it, Mr Westerham."

"That's right. Finish that bottle before you go. Now I fancy you'll be wanting to see me some time tomorrow."

"I'll run over in the morning, sir."

Westerham smiled.

"I don't think you will. I fancy you'll be doing something else. Later on, say. I'll stay at home, and expect you. By the way, is the policeman here on the 'phone?"

"Yes—he is."

"That's all right. You may want to communicate with him. And, Ringwood?"

"Yes, sir."

"It isn't necessary to take out a warrant before you arrest a man on a murder charge, is it?"

"Certainly not, sir. That's only done in the story books."

"I thought so. Well, that's all. It may sound very queer, but I've method in my madness, all the same."

The "chug-chug" of Ringwood's motor cycle gradually died away. Westerham locked the front door, and went up to bed.

"I wonder!" he said to himself, as he began to undress. "But we shall know tomorrow."

CHAPTER 17

It was just after breakfast the next morning that Froome, the village policeman, called to see the Vicar. He consulted his invariable note book, and announced, with his measured, routine voice,

"I'm instructed to inform you, sir, that you will be wanted to give evidence at eleven o'clock on Saturday morning next at the court at Sydbury in the case against Manoel Garcia, charged with the murder of Felix Nayland on the fifth of August—ultimo."

He rolled the last work out, apparently with great satisfaction, as if it thoroughly clinched his message.

"Very well," replied Westerham.

"And," went on Froome, producing a slip of paper, "I am further instructed to serve you with this subpoena, relative to the same—aforesaid."

Again it was the last word which was emphasized with due importance.

Then Constable Froome, having effected his official announcement, resolved himself into ordinary humanity.

"And I hope he'll get his deserts, sir!" he exclaimed. "And that's a rope with a noose at the end of it. I ain't vindictive, sir, but I don't hold with murder."

"I hope none of us do," replied the Vicar, mildly.

The Policeman still lingered.

"Do you remember, sir," he said, "when I first appeared on this case? By those pools of water it was, and Mr Nayland was lying there with that knife in his back. What did I say then, sir? Didn't I tell you Sergeant Ringwood was the right man for the job?"

"You did, yes."

"And I was right, you see, sir. Lord bless you, Ringwood's got more arteries in his little finger than ordinary persons like me and you have in their whole bodies. Not but what *I* didn't tumble to a thing or two all the same—but I can't talk about that. Ringwood's a demon—you never know where to have him. Why," and he scratched his head thoughtfully, "even *I* can't tell what he's driving at sometimes."

And a puzzled look came over his face.

"But I mustn't stay gossiping, sir. I've got to serve a similar subpoena on Mr Burt—at 'The Pleasaunce,' and then—there's other work to be done. Good morning, sir."

And, saluting the Vicar, he strode off, with an importantly mysterious bearing.

Westerham's lips curled in a little smile. He knew, by what was happening, that Ringwood had lost no time in taking certain suggestions that his letter contained. Presently he put on his hat and went out, on parochial business.

He took a short cut by the lane at the back of his Vicarage. This lane led to the main road and station on the right, and to a farm house and group of cottages on the left. And Westerham wanted to pay a call at the aforesaid farm. When he came out into the lane, he was almost opposite the little gate that opened into the wood through which the private path led to "The Pleasaunce." Near this gate, seated on the bank beside the lane, was a man engaged in reading a newspaper and smoking a pipe, a very ordinary looking individual, in a dark suit and soft, grey hat. He looked up at the Vicar as the latter passed by, but said nothing.

Having paid his visit to the farm, Westerham's next place of call was the post office. This stood in the upper part of Coppleswick, on the further side of "The Pleasaunce," and to reach it there was no need to retrace his steps along the lane. He took a short, direct cut across the fields from the farm, and came out into the upper main road. It was from this road that the narrow drive, the main entrance to "The Pleasaunce," struck off at right angles, nearly opposite the post office.

Froome, the policeman, was standing in the road just outside the post office, apparently engaged in making a solemn study of village life. He saluted the Vicar. The latter went in, bought the postal order for which he had come, glancing at a clock that hung on the wall as he did so. Five minutes past one. He lunched at half past, and had one more call to pay. As he came out he saw George Allen, the gardener's lad at "The Pleasaunce" coming into the main road from the narrow drive, presumably to his dinner.

A parishioner came up just then and the Vicar passed a few minutes with him in conversation. When he *did* make a start, glancing across the road, he noticed that George Allen was talking to Froome, and that the latter was tilting his helmet back with one hand and in the act of extracting his fat note book from his pocket with the other.

The Vicar went on. His next call was at the station, where he wanted to have a word with the station master about his forthcoming choir excursion. Coppleswick Railway Station, as has been said before, was a small one, but it was on the main line, and quite a number of trains stopped there in the course of the day, for the village was increasing, and many Sydbury people, tradesmen and others, had their residence there, while quite a respectable handful of men, like Garforth, went up to London daily.

To reach the station, he had to make a circuit, by the main road. He transacted his business with the station master, who was on the platform. There was, also, another individual there, in a grey suit and straw hat, sitting on one of the seats reading a book.

And, Westerham, as he walked on to his Vicarage, smiled once more. For he had observed several items of interest during that morning walk.

It was a little past four that afternoon that a car drove up to the Vicarage, and the Superintendent and Detective Sergeant Ringwood, the latter in plain clothes, got out. And when they came into the study Westerham knew by the triumphant gleam in the detective's eyes before he spoke a word, what had happened.

"Well?" he asked.

"Quite right, sir. There isn't a doubt about it, so the Scotland Yard expert says. I told you the print from the knife was faint and blurred, but there's enough to go by. How the dickens you managed it gets me, though, sir!"

Westerham smiled.

"I told you last night that Chateau Yquan might help, didn't I?"

"I don't follow it all yet, Mr Westerham," broke in the Superintendent, "but from what Ringwood tells me we're greatly indebted to you—though we shan't make that public if you don't wish it. You must tell us more afterwards. But there's quite enough with this finger print business to get to work at once—I don't want to delay."

"Now?" asked Westerham, significantly.

The Superintendent nodded.

"Certainly," he replied, "wouldn't you like to come, too? As a matter of fact that's why we called here first. A bit out of order, perhaps—but we almost reckon you one of us."

"All right," said the Vicar, who was really as keen as mustard, "I'll come."

"Then, if you don't mind, sir," said Ringwood, "we'll take the short cut—your back way, and through the wood."

As the three men crossed the lane at the back of the Vicarage, the individual who had been seated on the bank in the morning was still there, and came sauntering up, hands in pockets. Ringwood, without speaking, gave him a beckoning nod, and he followed them.

"One of our men, Mr Westerham," he exclaimed.

"Yes, I know," retorted Westerham, quietly, "and Froome's kicking his heels somewhere near the front entrance still, I suppose, and the other fellow must have made a complete study of the station by this time. So you took my hint?"

"Yes, but I'm not clear yet exactly what it meant."

"I'll tell you later."

The four men made their way along the grassy path through

the thick portion of the wood. Presently it opened out a bit, and they were just nearing the Diana's Pool, when Ringwood, who was leading, suddenly stopped, and said, in a low voice,

"Look!"

Through the trees they caught sight of a man coming across the open paddock between them and the house, a man who was walking at a good round pace, carrying a gladstone bag in his hand.

"By George!" whispered the Inspector, as the four men instinctively drew back under cover, "he's doing a bunk."

"Wouldn't have got far!" growled the man who had been in the lane all day.

"Nemesis!" exclaimed the Vicar, as he suddenly realised that they were standing almost upon the spot where the murder had taken place.

The oncomer could not see them. He had left the paddock now and was walking along one of the narrow grass paths which wound in and out the tree trunks, leading to Diana's Pool.

"There's a train to London at five ten," whispered Detective Sergeant Ringwood, and it sounded, to Westerham's ears, extremely banal in that tense moment.

The man came on. He reached the narrow path between the two pools, had almost passed between them, when Ringwood seemed to glide from the undergrowth which was hiding them, quietly, without excitement—so quietly that he was almost within arm's length of the other, when the latter stopped short.

"James Burt!" the voice was as quiet and self-contained as his movements had been, though what he said was the bluntest sentence, "James Burt, I arrest you on the charge of murdering Felix Nayland!"

Burt, taken absolutely by surprise, dropped the bag he was carrying. Before he could find words in which to reply, Ringwood suddenly, as it were springing into life, made a rapid movement towards him. There came what looked like a whirling of hands, with a glint of steel, a sudden click. At the same instant the Superintendent and the plain clothes man stepped out into the open, and Burt, handcuffed, found himself facing the three of them.

"And I caution you that anything you say, will be taken down and may be used in evidence."

Formal, uncompromising, yet all the time with the British spirit of fair play—such is an arrest by an English police officer.

Burt, recovering himself a little, exclaimed, "What do you mean? Do you imagine I should kill my own master? You're making a great mistake, Mr Ringwood—and you'll have to explain it."

"Burt!"

Afterwards Westerham used to say he was ashamed of himself at the recollection of that moment. Just then, parson or no parson, he was tasting that terrible excitement born of a man hunt, the latent savage, call it that if you like, that lurks beneath the veneer of polished civilisation. At the moment of his arrest he had moved from the others—it might have been an innate melodramatic instinct—he always said, afterwards, that he seemed to move and act mechanically. Psychologists would probably put it down to the influence of his subconscious mind, on which was indelibly impressed the theory that he had been working out. Be it what it may, he was standing by the tree on the further side of the upper pool, by the spot on which Ringwood had found the impression of Nayland's footprints.

"Burt!"

The man turned. He saw, across the pool, Westerham standing there, his right arm pointing upwards, his fist clenched, his eyes fixed upon the butler. And, as Burt looked at him, he suddenly flung his arm forward with a jerk, opening his hand as he did so.

James Burt positively flinched for the moment, then he yelled, "You devil!" and darted forward, raising his manacled hands. But strong arms restrained him, though it took all three of them to keep him back. Then he suddenly subsided.

"What are you going to do with me?" he growled.

"You are coming with me to Sydbury," replied the Superintendent, "When you are there you will be charged and then you are at liberty to make any statement you please. But you're not obliged to, you know."

"Can I consult a lawyer?"

"Certainly. Now, please! I've got a car waiting." They retraced their way through the wood, the Superintendent and the plain clothes man with Burt between them, Westerham and Ringwood following, the latter carrying Burt's bag.

"I'm going to remain for a bit," said Ringwood, in a low tone of voice to Westerham, "I shall have to get Miss Nayland to let me search his room, you know. And I want a good deal of explanation from you, sir."

"You shall have it."

Arrived at the Vicarage the Superintendent and his man waited with their prisoner while their car—which was driven by another policeman, ran to the station to fetch the "shadower" there, and then on to the village with a message to Froome that he could consider himself off duty. When it returned, it was to take Burt into Sydbury.

Before they started however, Westerham had a private word for the Superintendent.

"You may find it interesting," he said, "to give Burt's hair a good washing with soap and water—and then see if Manoel Garcia recognises him!"

"Why?" asked the Superintendent.

"Because I don't think his name is James Burt at all. I fancy it is Jasper Beech," replied Westerham, drily.

"The Dickens!" exclaimed the Superintendent, "that would explain a lot."

"It explains everything," retorted Westerham.

CHAPTER 18

"You'd better have another glass of my Chateau Yquan," said Westerham to the detective. "I'll open a fresh bottle. It was only the last evening I opened the other—for Burt to sample."

"That's how you got his finger prints on that little tumbler you gave me last night, eh, sir?"

"That's it. He never suspected for a moment what I was up to."

"But how did you happen to suspect him?" asked Ringwood.

"I'm going to tell you." He opened the drawer in his writing table, "I've got all the heads jotted down in their right sequence here, but, of course, it was a jigsaw at first."

"I think if I may say so, you're rather a wonder, Mr Westerham," said Ringwood, admiringly, as he took a sip of the Chateau Yquan.

"No, I'm not. It only meant a little close observation and ordinary common sense, nothing more. Also an open mind. You see, you had concentrated, first on Garcia and then on O'Calligan, but I couldn't make up my mind about either—especially Garcia. The only thing that still puzzles me about him is why he left that five pound note on Anstey."

"He didn't, Mr Westerham. We've known that a long time, and I may as well tell you now. It was that that began breaking down the case against him—that, and the finger prints."

And he told the Vicar about Perrivale's letter.

"I see," replied Westerham, "Well, that clears up *that* point. And now for the pieces of my puzzle."

"When did you first suspect Burt, sir?"

"I really can't say. Not definitely till two days ago. I began by noticing something queer about him, though I couldn't connect it with anything at the time. We had a fete the other day and I saw Burt win three packets of cigarettes—ordinary gaspers—in a competition. And when I spoke to him about it he said they were of no use to him—and he gave them back. Half an hour or so afterwards I came across him in the act of rolling a cigarette, and I noticed that he didn't lick the edge before he lighted it. *He tucked in the ends*, see? Now, you remember that ungummed paper, by the pool? Well, of course I'd got that at the back of my mind all the time. I knew already that Nayland didn't smoke cigarettes, and afterwards Valdez, who saw me here, let out that Garcia didn't smoke at all. Did *you* do anything more about that paper, Ringwood?"

"I found the stump of a cigarette made with the same sort of paper—the end tucked in—lying on the ground in the marquee on the day of the murder. But I connected it with Garcia—afterwards I had a notion O'Calligan might have smoked it."

"Both assumptions very natural, of course. Well, to go on with my story. I'd better give you the big clue first, because I really worked back from that. One thing that always confused me when I tried to piece matters out was why Nayland was standing by that tree on the further side of the upper pool."

"I've often tried to figure that out," replied Ringwood, "there were his footprints plain enough. He *was* standing there all right."

"No he wasn't," replied Westerham, with a smile.

"But they were his footprints?"

"Perfectly true."

"Then, what the dickens—?"

"Look here. Read this letter. It came with some of Nayland's clothes which his sister sent me for our Jumble Sale—it's from Miss Nayland herself. I was very busy at the time and did not take in the significance of it. It must have dropped accidentally into one of my drawers, here, and I only came across it again two days ago. But you read it, Sergeant."

And the detective read as follows,

MY DEAR VICAR:

I am sending you a parcel containing some of my dear brother's belongings for the stall at the Jumble Sale. I know you won't think me heartless in parting with my poor brother's clothes so soon, but I feel I should like them to serve some useful purpose. There are two or three quite good suits, and some underlinen, etc. I would have sent you also his boots and shoes, but he has been in the habit of giving his old ones to Burt, whom they fit, and for sentimental reasons I have followed his example.

Yours very sincerely,

ALICE NAYLAND.

"See?" asked Westerham curtly, when Ringwood had read the letter.

"By George, yes, I do, sir! That puts a very different light on things. You mean that Burt was standing behind that tree—wearing a pair of his master's boots?"

"That's it. That was the inference I went upon, at any rate. And, you see, it fitted in at once with the cigarette paper, and what I'd noticed at the fete. You can verify it—apart from Miss Nayland's letter, I fancy."

"Oh, I think so. I have Mr Nayland's boots that he was wearing that day. And I shall compare them with Burt's—and any we may find in his bag and in his room."

"Quite so. Well, to go on. This led me to other matters. I consulted my notes, and I found that when I strolled out of the house, at a quarter to six, when the concert was going on, I took shelter presently in the marquee. The waiters were there, packing up. While I was there Burt came in, and asked me if he could get me anything. I *did* notice at the time, but attached no particular importance to it then, that his shoulders were quite wet with rain. Now, if he had only been over to the house, they wouldn't have been wet like that. But I saw, when I put the jigsaw together, that he must have just returned from the wood, and, as he crossed the paddock, would stand a chance of getting drenched. That enabled me to fix the time of the murder—just before six, and another clue came along which showed me, so I believe, exactly how it was done."

"How was it done, Mr Westerham?"

"It's pure conjecture, of course. But it all fits in exactly. I'll give you my idea of it, and, to do that, I must go off on a tangent. I've already told your Superintendent that I fancy James Burt is not James Burt at all, he's Jasper Beech—the man who was associated with O'Calligan out in San Miguel."

"Good Lord, Mr Westerham, how do you make that out?"

"In several ways. Partly because of something that Señor Valdez told me about Beech—I'll mention that in a minute or two—and partly because it's about the only thing that explains the motive of the crime—and I'll refer to that presently. I was lunching with Miss Nayland last week—I'd been to help her with some of her brother's affairs, and when Burt leaned over my shoulder when serving me at the table I noticed he hadn't shaved that morning, which was very careless of him, because the tiny bit of beard that he had grown was *fair*—and his hair was black. Anyhow, with all this on my mind, I ran up to London yesterday and enquired at the offices of the Blue Diamond line. They were able to tell me that Burt had made his first voyage as steward on the "Pelican"—the boat Nayland came home in, you remember. They were short of a steward at Rio, and took him on there. They were also able to tell me that they had ascertained afterwards that he was an undesirable character, and that he was getting away from South America in general and San Miguel in particular when he signed on. And I think you'll be able to corroborate that from the Rio police."

"I shall see these people at the Blue Diamond Line offices tomorrow, Mr Westerham."

"Good. Well now, here you are. We can reconstruct the whole thing now. Remember that Garcia had solemnly sworn to kill Beech on sight, when he met with him. And Beech knew it. There were others, I daresay, who were after Beech as well, but there was no one he feared more. Well, Garcia comes to the garden party, we know all about that. His beard was evidently a poor disguise, for Nayland soon recognised him. And so, you may depend upon it, did Beech—probably when the Band went into the marquee for tea. Beech would get the fright of his life, because he would naturally think that Garcia had traced him to Coppleswick. He may have carried a knife on him, he may have run over to the house to get it, but he had it with him when he followed Garcia and Nayland into the wood. I don't suppose he went further than the pools. He probably waited there—behind that tree—to see what was going to happen when Garcia and Nayland came back—for they had gone into the wood, you remember. He rolled a cigarette, dropping a stray paper from the wad of papers as he did so.

"Then he saw Nayland coming back alone, and Nayland was wearing the bandsman's green jacket. I'm sure Garcia told the truth about that. Remember, it was very dark and gloomy under those trees, and it was perfectly natural that he should mistake Nayland for Garcia. And he knew it was either his life or Garcia's if they met. The *real* setting of the crime is South America, not an English garden. He did exactly what he'd already done in South America, he waited, hidden, till Nayland was in the middle of that path between the pools, his back to him and then —"

"And then, yes, I see," said the detective, as Westerham paused, "then he rushed up behind him and stabbed him."

"Nothing of the kind," retorted Westerham, "he stood still where he was."

"How did he kill him then?"

"Quite simply. He threw the knife at him—across the pool."

"Whew!" whistled Ringwood, "what makes you think that, Mr Westerham?"

"Two reasons. First because that was the way Valdez told me he murdered one of Garcia's sons, and secondly because I saw him give an exhibition of the art of knife throwing myself."

"Where?"

"Well, it wasn't exactly knife throwing, but it amounted to the same thing. At the fete. There was a dart throwing game—at a target marked with numbers—three darts for two pence, and a packet of cigarettes if you made above a certain score. Three times I saw him throw three darts, and each time those darts stuck in the three highest numbers in the board. That's when he won those cigarettes I told you of. I didn't notice it at the time, I mean I didn't attach any meaning to it, apart from his extraordinary skill, but when Valdez told me he'd killed a man by throwing a knife at him—well, I put two and two together—and I fancy they make four."

"Is that why you made that queer motion with your hand just now—by the pool, sir?"

"It is. I ought not to have done so. It was a sudden impulse and I can't imagine what I was thinking of."

"No wonder he called you a devil, Mr Westerham," exclaimed the detective, and there was admiration in the tone of his voice, "I'm beginning to think you're uncanny myself."

"Not at all," replied the Vicar, "I take credit for nothing but my hobby of observing things, and getting to the root of them. Think it over, and you'll see everything was quite simple—it only wanted putting together. I don't claim to be a Sherlock Holmes, and my deductions are only commonplace—there's no brilliance in them. Besides, I was actuated by a motive all the time. I wanted to get hold of poor Nayland's murderer, certainly, and I also wanted to get someone out of rather a trying ordeal."

The detective thought a moment.

"You mean Miss Garforth?"

"I do. You may as well know that Miss Garforth and I are engaged to be married. Naturally I wanted to rescue her from a very unpleasant position—and the rest of her family too."

"I understand, sir. I was present when O'Calligan made his statement to us, and I know he wouldn't have spared her had it come to a trial. He's too brutally callous. Well, we shall have to let him go, I suppose, for we've nothing against him that I can see. And Garcia, too. Yes, sir—I don't think Miss Garforth's name will be dragged into this now. And I'd like to congratulate you, Mr Westerham."

"Thanks very much."

"One thing more," went on Ringwood, "because I'm not quite clear about it?"

"Yes?"

"Why did you ask, in the letter you gave me last night, to serve you and Burt—or rather Beech—with subpoenas this morning, and then to have him shadowed?"

"Oh, first because I thought it might allay any suspicion on his part that you were moving against him—on my instigation. I knew him to be exceedingly crafty, of course, and, after he left me last evening, he might have turned matters over in his mind and have guessed my little ruse in getting his finger prints on that glass. But, as long as he knew he was wanted as a *witness*, he would be likely to fancy himself free from any suspicion. At the same time, however, I imagined that directly he was certain that he would have to appear against Garcia, he would make preparations for leaving Coppleswick. That's why I suggested he should be watched."

"Yes, I see, Mr Westerham. And yet I don't entirely follow you, even yet. Why should being definitely cited as a witness make him abscond?"

"Because he was never going to face Garcia—he dare not risk it. Several times he asked me when I thought he would have to give his evidence in the police court, and that set me thinking. Remember, he has never yet been confronted with Garcia. He took care to keep out of the way at the adjourned inquest, when Garcia was there. He was afraid of being recognised. And you told him—as you told me—that he wouldn't be wanted the first and second times Garcia was brought before the magistrates. His plan, I think, was to hang on here till the last moment. You can figure it out like this. Burt—or rather Beech—was in a pretty desperate state. He had fled for his life from San Miguel and he had an atrociously bad record. He wanted a refuge for a long time till things had blown over. That's why, probably, he jumped

201

at Nayland's offer to take him on as butler. Here, in a quiet country village, he could lie low for a time with perfect safety. Even after he had killed Nayland it was safer for him to remain on at 'The Pleasaunce' for the very fact of leaving suddenly would have aroused suspicion. But he'd made up his mind to get away before he had to appear against Garcia. As I said before, he dare not risk *that!*"

"He'll have to face him now," replied Ringwood, with a grim smile, "only the positions will be reversed—Garcia in the witness box and Beech in the dock. Now, sir, may I have your notes on the case?"

"Certainly. Here they are, jotted down in order. I make you a present of them with pleasure. But we'd better just go through them first."

It was some time before the two men had finished—and then Westerham's telephone bell rang. He took up the receiver, and listened, his eyes shining with interest. When he put it down, he said to Ringwood,

"Just as I thought—that was the Superintendent speaking, and he hasn't lost any time. Garcia has identified Burt as Beech, and there was a bit of a scene over it. Garcia flew at him and got him by the throat before they guessed what he was up to—and they had quite a job to drag him off. Also the Superintendent says they've given the prisoner a preliminary wash—sort of shampoo, I imagine—and the water in the basin was black when they'd finished."

"Umph! that settles it," said Ringwood. He glanced at his watch.

"There's a train back to Sydbury I want to catch," he said, "but I must run over to 'The Pleasaunce' first and have a look at this fellow's room."

"I'll come with you," replied the Vicar. "I'd better break the news to Miss Nayland. I don't suppose Beech took leave of her before he slipped out the back way—Yes? Come in!"

"Constable Froome is in the hall, sir," said the maid who entered the room, "he wishes to speak to Mr Ringwood."

"Show him in here," said Westerham.

Froome came in, in full official bearing, helmet tucked under his arm.

"Yes?" asked Ringwood, "what is it?"

"Can I have a word with you, Sergeant?"

And he glanced significantly at Westerham.

"Is it anything to do with Burt?" asked Ringwood.

"Yes."

"All right then. You can say what you have to say before Mr Westerham."

Again the Policeman glanced—and a little unfavourably, too —at the Vicar, but obeyed orders, nevertheless. He took out his note book,

"A matter of report, Sergeant," he said.

Ringwood nodded.

"Go on."

Constable Froome cleared his throat and read as follows,

"I was on duty this morning, according to my instructions, in the upper main road at Coppleswick, near the post office. At seven minutes past one I was accosted by George Allen, under gardener at 'The Pleasaunce' who told me he had a communication to make touching the murder of Mr Felix Nayland on the fifth of August ultimo. I cautioned him in the usual manner.

"Allen stated that he had been questioned by Detective Sergeant Ringwood at the time of the murder, that the Sergeant had asked him if he had observed any suspicious characters that day, and that he had said he had not. Had he seen one of the bandsmen or Mr Nayland going towards, or into the wood? Had he seen anyone going there while the concert was being performed in the hall? To which he had replied that he had not."

"Allen then made the following statement, which I wrote down. He said, 'I did not tell Sergeant Ringwood something which I wish to say now. I thought when I answered his questions that was all I was called upon to say. And it did not occur to me that what I saw was of importance. I have now been told'—he refused to tell me who told him" Froome said, parenthetically, "'I have now been told that I should be a liar even if I didn't say what I wasn't asked to say'—those were his exact words, Sergeant—'I will say it now. On the afternoon of the party at Mr Nayland's I was on duty in the field where the cars were parked, the said field being adjacent.'"

"Can't imagine George using *that* word," said the Vicar to himself, with a smile.

"'Being adjacent to the wood and the paddock at the back of the house. Just before six o'clock'—he knew the hour, so he said, because he heard the church clock strike soon afterwards," commented the policeman, "'just before six o'clock I was standing by the low hedge dividing the field from the paddock. It was raining hard and I was sheltering under a tree. I saw a man coming from the wood and running across the paddock towards the house. The man was James Burt, the butler at 'The Pleasaunce.' I attached no importance to the incident,'"

The Vicar smiled again at this conventional phrase.

"'Knowing that Burt had his duties to perform at the party. It never occurred to me to inform Sergeant Ringwood. That is all I wish to say.'"

Constable Froome closed his pocket book; he was standing stiffly upright, a typical representative of a Force which may act at times in rigid routine, but which is always dogged and persistent—in spite of frequent criticism.

"That concludes George Allen's statement," he said.

Detective Sergeant Ringwood turned to Westerham,

"And that clinches it, I think!" was his comment.

*

And it *did!*

THE END

VICTOR L. WHITECHURCH CRIME FICTION BIBLIOGRAPHY

1. *Thrilling Stories of the Railway* (C. Arthur Pearson, London 1912/no US edition/Spitfire Publishers 2024). Short story collection.

2. *The Templeton Case: A Detective Story* (John Long, London 1924/Edward J. Clode, New York 1924/Spitfire Publishers, 2022).

3. *The Crime at Diana's Pool* (T. Fisher Unwin, London 1927/ Duffield and Company, New York 1927/Spitfire Publishers 2024).

4. *Shot on the Downs* (T. Fisher Unwin, London 1927/Duffield and Company, New York 1928/Spitfire Publishers, 2024).

5. *Mixed Relations* (Ernest Benn, London 1928). US title: *The Robbery at Rudwick House* (Duffield and Company, New York 1929).

6. *Murder at the Pageant* (W. Collins and Sons, London 1930/ Duffield and Company, New York 1931).

7. *Murder at the College* (W. Collins and Sons, London 1932). US title: *Murder at Exbridge* (Dodd, Mead and Company, New York 1932).

Printed in Great Britain
by Amazon